"Making A Point Here, Doc?"

"I'm here at your request, Mr. Cade. Beyond that, I have no point to make."

"Ah." Jackson Cade's smile was mocking as his gaze lingered over the slight décolletage of her gown. As mocking, as disparaging, his gaze traveled with exquisite thoroughness down the length of her slim, dark skirt to linger pointedly on scuffed boots.

"Then we're to believe you always make barn calls dressed like the Duchess of Belle Terre?" he murmured. "Or better still, that with a few paltry concessions to this call, we should understand you're slumming by coming to River Trace?"

Haley was determined not to allow him the satisfaction of seeing her react.

"We both know I've never made a visit here. We both know why. I've never come to River Trace because you never wanted me here."

Dear Reader,

Welcome to Silhouette Desire, where every month you'll find six passionate, powerful and provocative romances.

October's MAN OF THE MONTH is *The Taming of Jackson Cade*, part of bestselling author BJ James' MEN OF BELLE TERRE miniseries, in which a tough horse breeder is gentled by a lovely veterinarian. *The Texan's Tiny Secret* by Peggy Moreland tells the moving story of a woman in love with the governor of Texas and afraid her scandalous past will hurt him.

The exciting series 20 AMBER COURT continues with Katherine Garbera's *Some Kind of Incredible,* in which a secretary teaches her lone-wolf boss to take a chance on love. In *Her Boss's Baby,* Cathleen Galitz's contribution to FORTUNES OF TEXAS: THE LOST HEIRS, a businessman falsely accused of a crime finds help from his faithful assistant and solace in her virginal embrace.

Jacob's Proposal, the first book in Eileen Wilks' dynamic new series, TALL, DARK & ELIGIBLE, features a marriage of convenience between a beauty and a devastatingly handsome financier known as the Iceman. And Maureen Child's popular BACHELOR BATTALION marches on with *Last Virgin in California,* an opposites-attract romance between a tough, by-the-book marine drill instructor and a free-spirited heroine.

So celebrate the arrival of autumn by indulging yourself with all six of these not-to-be-missed love stories.

Enjoy!

Joan Marlow Golan

Joan Marlow Golan
Senior Editor, Silhouette Desire

Please address questions and book requests to:
Silhouette Reader Service
U.S.: 3010 Walden Ave., P.O. Box 1325, Buffalo, NY 14269
Canadian: P.O. Box 609, Fort Erie, Ont. L2A 5X3

The Taming of
Jackson Cade
BJ JAMES

Published by Silhouette Books

America's Publisher of Contemporary Romance

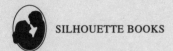 SILHOUETTE BOOKS

ISBN 0-373-76393-X

THE TAMING OF JACKSON CADE

Books by BJ James

Silhouette Desire

The Sound of Goodbye #332
Twice in a Lifetime #396
Shiloh's Promise #529
Winter Morning #595
Slade's Woman #672
A Step Away #692
Tears of the Rose #709
*The Man with the
  Midnight Eyes* #751
Pride and Promises #789
Another Time, Another Place #823
The Hand of an Angel #844
*Heart of the Hunter #945
*The Saint of Bourbon Street #951
*A Wolf in the Desert #956
†Whispers in the Dark #1081
†Journey's End #1106
†Night Music #1286
‡The Return of Adams Cade #1309
‡A Season for Love #1335
‡A Lady for Lincoln Cade #1369
‡The Taming of Jackson Cade #1393

Silhouette Intimate Moments

Broken Spurs #733

Silhouette Books

World's Most Eligible Bachelors
†*Agent of the Black Watch*

*Men of the Black Watch
†The Black Watch
‡Men of Belle Terre

BJ JAMES'

first book for Silhouette Desire was published in February 1987. Her second Desire title garnered for BJ a second Maggie, the coveted award of Georgia Romance Writers. Through the years there have been other awards and nominations for awards, including, from *Romantic Times Magazine,* Reviewer's Choice, Career Achievement, Best Desire, and Best Series Romance of the Year. In that time, her books have appeared regularly on a number of bestseller lists, among them Waldenbooks and *USA Today.*

On a personal note, BJ and her physician husband have three sons and two grandsons. While her address reads Mooreboro, this is only the origin of a mail route passing through the countryside. A small village set in the foothills of western North Carolina is her home.

FOREWORD

In the coastal Lowcountry of South Carolina, where the fresh waters of winding rivers flow into the sea, there is an Eden of unmatched wonders. In this mix of waters and along the shores by which they carve their paths, life is rich and varied. The land is one of uncommon contrasts, with sandy, seaswept beaches, mysterious swamps, teeming marshes bounded by ancient maritime forests. And a multitude of creatures that abide in each.

In this realm of palms and palmettos, estuaries and rivers, shaded by towering live oaks draped in ghostly Spanish moss, lies Belle Terre. Like an exquisite pearl set among emeralds and sapphires, with its name the small antebellum city describes its province. As it describes itself.

Belle Terre, beautiful land. A beautiful city.

A very proper, very elegant, beautiful city. A gift for the soul. An exquisite mélange for the senses. With ancient and grand structures in varying states of repair and disrepair set along tree-lined, cobbled streets. With narrow, gated gardens lush with such greenery as resurrection and cinnamon ferns. And all of it wrapped in the lingering scent of camellias, azaleas, jessamine, and magnolias.

Steeped in an aura of history, its culture and customs influenced by plantations that once abounded in the Lowcountry, as it clings to its past Belle Terre is a province of contradictions. Within its society one will find arrogance abiding with humility, cruelty with kindness, insolence with gentility, honor with depravity, and hatred with love.

As ever when the senses are whetted and emotions untamed, in Belle Terre there will be passion, romance, and scandal.

Prologue

In a rare moment of peace, unmindful of the blaze of light spilling through the barn door to lie like pale fire on the ground before him, Jackson Cade stood as rigid as a figure of stone.

In sudden, blessed quiet, his bleak gaze ranged over the land beyond. But he didn't see.

His mind was too full of turmoil and grief to appreciate how beautiful the acres of lush pasture were in moonlight. He didn't smell the perfume of a southern night drifting on a breeze that touched his heated skin in a cooling kiss.

Once he would have stood in this exact spot with a sense of pride in all he saw. For this was River Trace. His land, his home, and he'd made it what it was. But tonight there was no pride, no sense of accomplishment. Only the knowledge that he'd fought a fierce and frenzied battle...and failed.

Because of his failure and stubborn pride, a magnificent suffering creature would die. And with it his dreams.

Footsteps sounded behind him, a hand clasped his shoulder.

Jesse Lee, a trusted friend, an expert horseman, asked gruffly, "What are you doing standing here like this?"

A heavy shoulder lifted beneath the old cowboy's rough hand. "Wishing I could change things, I suppose."

Jessee nodded even though he knew the younger man wouldn't see. "I reckon we both wish we could change a lot of things. But fact is we can't. And there's no going back. Only forward."

Jackson laughed, a bitter, defeated sound. "How do I do that? Accomplishing what?"

"You do it by taking yourself into the house to make the phone call you've refused to consider." Jesse's fingers tightened on Jackson's shoulder. In compassion, in respect, in regret for a man too proud for his own good. "I can't say what it will accomplish, but it's a chance. And if it saves the poor, mad critter back there in that stall, or even if it only eases his suffering, what's the eating of a little crow in comparison?"

"You don't mince words, do you, old man?"

"Never have," Jesse drawled. "And just like you said, I'm too old to start."

Jackson nodded but didn't look away from the land.

This was more than River Trace. It was his dream. His life's work. The investment of all he had, his heart, his blood, his sweat and tears. After years of struggle, success beyond his wildest dreams was only a colt or two away. Colts that might not ever be. Unless a phone call could make the difference.

"Unless," he muttered, stepping into the moonlight.

"What does that mean?" the older man questioned, his arm falling to his side.

"Exactly that, Jesse. *Unless.*" Jackson walked, grimly, determinedly in a stilted pace toward the house. A tattered, historic treasure neglected in favor of barns and horses, but his.

"Where in thunder are you going, Jackson Cade?"

Without slowing his pace, Jackson called back over his shoulder, his voice grimly resigned, as stilted as his step. "To make a phone call. Eat some crow. Say a prayer."

"Care if I join you in the prayer part?"

"You do that." At the steps leading to the back door, Jackson swung about. Over the little distance, young eyes met old and held. "Thanks for coming tonight, Jesse. I know you tried."

"We both did, Jackson. What we could do just wasn't enough."

Jackson drew a long, harsh breath, nodded again, then turned away from the night to climb steps of stone.

The darkness of the house enveloped him, blocking him from sight, but the old cowhand still stood in the barn door. "Our bad luck was that your brother isn't here. The good is that there is someone else.

"*Call,*" Jesse urged softly in a whisper no ear but his would hear. "Take a chance. What you find just might be worth all the crow in the world."

One

The screams. She could still hear the screams.

Gripping the steering wheel, forgetting the incongruity of her stylishly perfect black dress and that her silver-blond hair was caught in a coil as perfect, Haley Garrett thrust a stiletto heel against the accelerator, sending the massive truck rocketing ever faster through darkness.

The hour was late—a harvest moon gleamed in a blue-black sky. But Haley gave no more thought to breathtaking Southern nights than she did to the glittering gala and the attractive man she'd deserted to come careening through the countryside.

Her riveted gaze rarely straying from the ribbon of unfamiliar asphalt, she thought of little but her destination, and the mystery awaiting her there. At last, as she passed through an open gate, thickets of pine and palm gave way to an avenue of oaks. Draped in ghostly moss, their massive limbs entwined over the lane in a leafy cathedral, sealing away the sky, the stars, the moon.

Beyond the gate there would be miles of carefully tended

fences. Fences guarding the many pastures of River Trace, premier horse farm of the South. She had heard the land was beautiful. She knew the horses bred there were extraordinary. But for Haley, the land was rent by the remembered screams of a single horse.

Hurt, maddened, its cries echoed unceasingly in her mind.

Even muffled over the telephone, the terrifying sounds had played a ghastly musical accompaniment to the desperate summons. No, worse than desperate. Jackson Cade would be worse than desperate to seek the help of Haley Garrett, newcomer to quaint Belle Terre, the city's newest Doctor of Veterinary Medicine.

The last of the trees flashed by, the truck burst into a flood of moonlight. Before her lay a midnight pastoral scene of South Carolina's lowcountry. With its shabby manor and sprawling lawns, it might have been taken from the pages of history.

"All that's lacking is the mint julep," Haley muttered, and was instantly contrite. Sarcasm was not normally a part of her attitude. But neither was she normally as anxious as now.

Driving on, she discovered the one jarring note was the main barn. Built in historic style, it was too obviously new. As light blazed from within the structure that, in time, would blend with its surroundings, Haley knew the interior would be uniquely modern.

Bringing the truck to a halt, she leaped to the ground. Pausing only to fling aside elegant sandals, she stamped her feet into practical boots and pulled on equally practical gloves.

Unconcerned by the paradox of her costume, but making a mental note that jeans and a sturdy shirt should be added to the supplies stored in the truck, she snatched up her medical bag. Thankful for the deep slit in her narrow skirt, Haley dashed for the barn, the thick grass muffling her footsteps until she stepped onto a cobblestone path by the entrance.

Blinded by the glare of lights, scarcely inside the open door, she paused. Shading her eyes with a hand at her forehead, she waited for her vision to adjust. In that little time Haley knew she'd been right. The barn was state-of-the art in horse breeding.

"Doc." A figure appeared at the end of the spotless hall. She recognized the voice before she could make out his face.

"Jesse." His name was her greeting. The familiar drawl belonged to Jesse Lee. The Arizona cowboy had come to the lowcountry to serve as foreman at nearby Belle Reve, where Gus Cade, patriarch of the Cade family, ruled with an iron will.

Given his vast knowledge of horses, and the proximity of the plantations, it wasn't surprising Jesse was here. Haley had expected that in the absence of Lincoln Cade, her veterinary partner, Jesse would be first choice at River Trace. As the horse quieted, she wondered where the rest of the staff could be.

Where *he* could be.

He. Jackson Cade, Lincoln's brother, third of Gus Cade's sons. The man who'd disliked her and rejected her help with his horses, until now. Until he, not Jesse, made the call.

Haley forced herself to proceed calmly. If she was not calm, she would be of little help. "How is he?" she asked, wondering if she meant the berserk horse or its owner. Remembering the tone of the call, she thought the question could apply to man or beast. "The situation sounded urgent. I came as quickly as I could."

"'Pears to me you came a mite too quick," Jesse drawled, with a glance flicking over her sleek black dress.

"Making a point here, *Doc?*" The second voice came from behind her. This drawl was deeper, colder. A far cry from Jesse's droll, good-natured teasing.

When Haley turned to face her accuser, his look was contemptuous, colder than his tone, leaving no room for misinterpretation of the unspoken insult. Though she tried not to react, it took all her strength to not respond in kind. Gleaning composure from lessons learned, refusing to be intimidated or provoked, her reply was unruffled. "I'm here at your request, Mr. Cade. Beyond that, I have no point to make."

"Ah." Jackson Cade's smile was mocking as his gaze lingered over the slight décolletage of her gown, reminding her that it afforded a glimpse of the tilt of her breasts and the shadowed cleft between them. As mocking, as disparaging, his gaze traveled with exquisite thoroughness down the length of her slim, dark skirt to linger pointedly on scuffed boots. As if to satisfy himself his message had been understood, he glanced at her hands and found them clenched within leather gloves.

"Then we're to believe you always make barn calls dressed like the Duchess of Belle Terre?" he murmured. "Or better still, that with a few paltry concessions to this call, we should understand you're slumming by coming to River Trace?"

The remark stung, as he'd intended. But Haley was determined to not allow him the satisfaction of seeing her react. "We both know I've never made a visit here. We both know why. I've never come to River Trace because you never wanted me here.

"Tonight, I came as I was. From the tone of your call and the sound of your horse, I felt it merited speed more than proper dress. Lincoln isn't here. In fact, as you well knew when you stooped to summoning me, he isn't even in the lowcountry. So, Mr. Horse Breeder par excellence, you would be wise to remember beggars can't be choosers." With a quick breath, she continued with false detachment, "Dressed to suit your personal code or not, unless I miss my guess, I'm all you have."

Jesse Lee smothered a strangled sound Haley could have sworn was a chuckle, yet she would not look away from Jackson Cade's narrowed stare to interpret it. Keeping his gaze, one that would have been gorgeous were it not so hard and cold, she drew herself to her tallest. A mistake, she realized as he abandoned the duel to let his attention sweep over the lifted thrust of her breasts as thoroughly as he had before.

Haley endured the ordeal by gathering her composure more closely around her, refusing this insufferable man the satisfaction of the blush that threatened. He'd called for help. The situation was unquestionably grave, yet he wasted precious time with this uncharacteristic, chauvinistic performance.

Uncharacteristic because Jackson Cade was known as a man who loved most women. Tall, short, fat, skinny, old, young, ugly or pretty, he loved them. Some without reservation. Others—ambitious, motivated career women such as she—he treated temperately, courteously, but from a coolly guarded distance.

That he cared little for her sort was patently clear. Yet even at his coolest he was, without fail, ever gallant, ever pleasant, ever respectful. Without fail, to all but the inexplicable pariah, Haley Garrett. For whom he reserved a special hostility. A vitriolic antipathy she didn't understand, escalating with each inadvertent encounter.

Even now, perversely, for reasons only he knew, in his dislike the need to humiliate her was stronger than his desperation. Which made no sense, for added to the legend was his even greater love of horses. Jackson Cade of River Trace was a breeder of some of the world's finest stock. One who spared neither time nor expense to insure their excellent care.

Despite an unmistakable distrust of his brother's partner in their veterinary practice, his attitude was senseless in the extreme. Haley couldn't begin to comprehend his motives or to fathom their origin. But, since it was doubtful he could ever address her in genial terms, much less explain her sins, she'd given up trying to understand this contrary, cantankerous Cade weeks ago.

Indeed, if it were only this frustrating man, she would turn on her booted heel, leaving River Trace in the dust and Jackson Cade to reap the consequences of his unbridled arrogance.

But the problem wasn't just the enigmatic Jackson Cade. There was the horse and its strange malady. In the midst of this standoff, troubled sounds had begun to drift from a distant stall. Proving, as Haley feared, the embattled quiet had been only the respite of overwhelming fatigue.

Because she couldn't turn her back on any hurting creature, she put resentment and quelled anger aside in favor of ethical prudence and compassion. "If it will make you feel better, I apologize for my costume, Mr. Cade. I was attending a dinner following a concert," she explained. "When you called, I considered the situation an emergency. I still do. If you'll let me, I'd like to help. To do that, I need to examine the horse while it's quiet. Which, from the sounds I'm hearing, won't be long."

Jackson Cade, whom she knew from his brothers had been trained from childhood to behave in a gentlemanly manner, had the grace to look ashamed of his behavior. But only for a single moment, for in the next he was covering the faltering of his dislike with a brusque gesture and a mocking bow. "Be my guest, Duchess. The problem with Dancer has stymied the best of us."

"So," Haley snapped with rare impatience, "as a last resort you decided to give me a shot at diagnosing."

"Something like that."

When he straightened from a sweeping bow worthy of a Knight of the Round Table, his blue gaze only vaguely mocking, eyes as blue waited for his. Ambushing him. Catching him off guard. In that naked glimpse Haley saw beyond the anger to hurt and fear. Jackson Cade was half mindless with worry because he cared so very much. His horses were more than a business. More than dollar signs. And like it or not, like *her* or not, Haley Garrett was truly his last resort.

"In that case," she responded, still keeping his gaze, "I'd best make this good, hadn't I?"

Turning away, she addressed the older man, who waited with an oddly pleased and knowing expression. But Haley couldn't be concerned with any more peculiar masculine behavior. "Jesse, if you would go with me to Dancer's stall…"

"I'll go." Jackson stepped closer. Even as the shortest of the Cades, he towered over her only a fraction less than a foot.

"No." He was so close, so imposing, she had to steel herself against the urge to step back. "Thank you, but no," she said in rephrase, hoping to avoid another confrontation. "I need a cool head. You're too emotionally involved to think clearly."

"This is my land, Dancer's my horse, *Doctor* Garrett." Eyes that could smile and warm female hearts were arctic blue.

"Your horse but my patient, Mr. Cade," Haley reminded him without returning his heavy-handed sarcasm. Without looking away from his piercing glare, she asked quietly, "Ready, Jesse?"

"Never readier." The slender cowhand pushed away from the wall where he'd leaned to watch the show. Now he was all business. "The hands took the other horses to pasture. Dancer's fit was catching. Part of what you heard over the phone was them, wild and getting wilder, though they didn't see what Dancer was imagining."

"A concert, you say?" Jesse changed subjects adroitly. Tossing the question over his shoulder, he led Haley down a corridor intersecting the main part of the barn. "I 'spose that means you had a date. A good-looking filly like you, dressed in pretty finery, be a shame if you didn't."

Whether there had or had not been a date or an escort was none of Jesse's business. But he was nearly as famous for his superstitions and harmless, gossipy curiosity as for his horse sense. For the latter, Haley admired and liked the wily old fox.

"Thank you for the compliment, Jesse. It's nice to know you think I'm a 'good-looking little filly.'" Smiling at the lumbering hitch in his step, she knew he was waiting for the punch line, and decided she wouldn't prolong the suspense. "And, yes, I had a date for the concert. For dinner, too."

Wide shoulders too heavy for his lanky form twitched, even as he resumed a smooth stride. "Guess it couldn't've been Daniel Corbett, since he would've been conducting."

This took prying to a ridiculous level, even for Jesse. But Haley had dealt with enough contention for one night. It wouldn't hurt to satisfy his determined curiosity. "It was chamber music, Jesse, not the orchestra. Daniel didn't conduct."

"Oh?"

Hearing mounting curiosity in the questioning word, wondering why he should care, she gripped the heavy bag, intending to shift it from one tired hand to the other hand. Before the move was completed, the bag was taken from her. Jackson had stepped forward. Medical bag in hand, he matched his stride to hers.

As she looked up at him, she realized that in the shadowed hall his features were haggard and incredibly weary. Excusing his insolence, in that moment her tender heart went out to him. But, certain the last thing this strong, hotheaded man wanted was sympathy, she turned her attention back to Jesse, who rattled on.

"I beg your pardon?" Haley hurried to catch up with the loquacious cowboy, and to keep Jackson at a comfortable distance. "Sorry, Jesse. I'm afraid I wasn't listening."

"Humph! You don't have to beg nothin' here, little girl. Considering Jackson's bark's worse than his bite, you don't have to be afraid, neither. What I was sayin' is, what with conducting and all, Daniel must be pretty interesting."

"Daniel's certainly interesting."

"I 'spose that short answer means you ain't gonna say just exactly who your date was?"

Wondering why she cared that Jackson was hearing this conversation, she brought it to an end. "As a matter fact, I'm not. I came to treat a horse, not to discuss my social life."

Grinning again at Jesse's grunt of frustration, she slowed her steps as he slowed. When he stopped at the bolted gate of a stall, in a gasping breath her grin was swept away.

Cade's Irish Dancer was known in informed circles as a magnificent stallion, a most valuable stud. Or he had been.

Haley had never been afforded the coveted opportunity to study him in the flesh. But she'd read about him, poring over his photographs in breeder and veterinary journals. Yet if she hadn't been told the exhausted creature cowering in the battered stall was the legendary horse, she wouldn't have believed it.

His coat was soaked with sweat and matted. His head

drooped, his tail hung dull and lifeless. Gone was the proud bearing of the much-sought-after stud that had once, no doubt, been as arrogant as his master. At a glance, he appeared to have lost a tremendous amount of weight. But given the short duration of his seizure, she knew it was likely severe dehydration.

Though it didn't explain Jackson's hostility toward her, Dancer's condition was cause enough for his mood.

"Jackson," she whispered, oblivious in her alarm that she called his given name. "How long has he been like this?"

"It began several hours ago." He waited a pace behind her. "The onset was like this, first lethargy then a few minutes of erratic behavior. Dancer's temperamental. It seemed like a fit of exceptionally bad humor at first. Then the madness started. We tried all we knew to calm him. Finally, both Jesse and I— and even all the hands—exhausted every avenue."

"Tell me." Haley's racing mind searched for answers. "Tell me everything. Don't leave out the smallest detail."

It was Jackson who answered, which was only natural. Dancer was his horse, the greatest source of his livelihood. More than that, the stallion's anguish was his anguish. When he finished explaining every treatment, she found he'd been thorough and practical. His mind quick, he was well organized and sensible. More reasons to be puzzled by his reaction to her.

Mulling over all he'd said, Haley nodded. Thinking hard as she studied the horse that was a pitiful remnant of the awesome creature he'd been, something nagged at her. Something Jesse had said, recalled briefly by Jackson's explanation. But in the shock and duress it had slipped from her mind.

"But what?" Out of habit, with no sign of vanity, she absently tucked a slipping hairpin into place. "Jesse!"

"Yes, ma'am. Still here."

"What was it you said?" Closing her eyes, as if blocking out her surroundings would bring the elusive thought within reach, she muttered, "Something about the other horses."

"I don't recall the order, but it was something about the

other horses reacting to Dancer, and the hands taking them to pasture.'' Sliding back his broad-brimmed hat, Jesse peered at her from the shadows cast by overhead lights. ''Does that help?''

Haley took a closer look at the stall, hoping for the spark of the thought. The effort changed nothing. She was as confounded as Jesse or Jackson.

Jackson? When had she begun to think of the stiff-necked man as Jackson? she wondered. Especially since it was unlikely they would ever be on a first-name basis as she was with his brothers Adams and Jefferson, who didn't avoid her.

Abandoning thoughts of the stubborn, arrogant Cade, returning to the elusive memory that teased at her mind, she admitted honestly, ''Maybe it will help. Then again, maybe not. Perhaps the thought was too far-fetched to stick.''

''Jesse said one other thing.'' Jackson came to stand by her, resting his arms on the stall door. In close proximity, mixed with the scent of hay and horse, Haley breathed in a pleasant woodsy fragrance that suited a man like Jackson. Except, what did she know of the kind of man he was? Or what would suit him?

In that rare moment, regret that he resented and disliked her so adamantly surfaced. In more amenable circumstances, she believed he would have been a gentleman, a man she could admire. One whose friendship she would value.

A pipe dream. It took two to make a friendship. Of all the emotions rampant between them, friendship was not one of them. Nor would it ever be. Unaware of her melancholy sigh, or that Jackson looked at her with something in his eyes that would have shocked her, focusing on the horse, Haley asked, ''What was it?''

Jackson had lost the thread of concentration. Brows only a little darker than his auburn hair lifted in question. '''It?''''

''Sorry.'' This was her night for apologies. ''I didn't mean to speak in riddles. Just wondering aloud what else Jesse said.'' She glanced at the cowhand, but he shrugged. Jesse had no answer or had delegated that responsibility to the younger man.

"What probably struck you as odd," Jackson volunteered again, "was his comment that the other horses weren't seeing what Dancer was imagining."

"Imagining?" She looked into eyes bearing no shred of anger. "Jesse thought the horse was imagining something?" Before either man could respond, she questioned Jackson. "Did *you?*"

"At the time, I didn't think of anything but preventing Dancer from hurting himself." Unconsciously, he brushed a roughened finger over the start of a bruise. Tomorrow he would have a colorful cheek, maybe a shiner. "Now that I remember Jesse saying it, yes, Dancer acted as if he was hallucinating. Maybe having a sort of seizure, which is ridiculous."

Hallucinations. Seizure. Induced by an exotic foreign substance? She'd seen it once before. The horse died, because the diagnosis had been made postmortem. If she was lucky… "Jesse, get me a syringe. Jackson, take my bag to a better light."

When both had done as she'd asked—she was working so quickly and thinking so hard—she hadn't realized she had given orders. Or that Jackson Cade had obeyed without question. When the syringe was prepared, she stopped to explain. "I think I've seen this before. If I'm right and I move quickly enough, we can save your Dancer. But you have to realize this is little more than a wild guess, a gamble. Luck of the draw, so to speak.

"If we had time for tests…"

"Which we don't," Jesse reminded her grimly.

In a regretful tone she warned, "If I'm wrong…"

"What you try could kill him." Oddly, as if he would spare her the grief of the words, Jackson stated the inescapable truth.

"Yes," she admitted, for there was no other answer.

"In this condition, he'll die if you don't try," Jesse put in, but Haley and Jackson were concentrating so intently on each other, neither heard. Neither needed to hear, for they knew.

"Last ditch," Jackson murmured.

"So it would seem. But Dancer's strong…there's a chance this could run its course before his heart gives out."

"No," he disagreed. "You didn't see him. Even if the next seizure is lighter, he won't survive it."

"Then will you trust me? Will you take the risk that I'm right?" Haley knew she faced the challenge of her career. As she'd warned, anything she did from this point on would be sheer guesswork. But with every other avenue exhausted, guesswork was all they had. All there was time for before another onset of Dancer's madness. Dancer's deliberately induced madness.

Haley caught a startled breath. *Deliberately induced?* Certainty came out of nowhere. But every intuition shouted *deliberate.* The word resounded in her mind like an echoing bell.

She knew little of the operation at River Trace, still less of its stubborn and scornful proprietor. Stubborn and scornful with her, she amended, for she knew his reputation as a laughing, flirting, kindhearted gentleman. Once, long ago, she'd known his gentleness. Times change, people change. Perhaps the young man who had been kind to a younger, obviously forgotten Haley Garrett, had changed. Perhaps he'd made enemies. Vicious enemies.

A concept she understood all too well. One not beyond the realm of possibility. After all, Jackson Cade had certainly done his best to make an enemy of her.

Dancer tossed his head, then staggered and whickered, a prelude to the screams that had brought her here. "Imagining," she whispered in a troubled tone, more certain than ever that she was right. There was hope for the horse now, but little time.

Laying a hand on the stall door, she started to enter when a hard, calloused hand covering hers stopped her. "Don't," Jackson said. "Whatever this is, it comes in stages. At his worst, he's too dangerous for you to take this risk. I'm sorry."

True regret flickered over his craggy, attractive face, startling Haley. Before she could protest that this was her job and that this was neither the first nor the last time she would face a dangerous creature, his clasp tightened, his fingers circling the back of her hand and her palm.

"I shouldn't have interrupted your evening, Duchess." This time the name lacked the sting it had carried before. If this hadn't been Jackson, if he hadn't proven time and again he had little use for her as a vet or a person, it could have been a nickname. The sort a friend might bestow on a friend.

Friends? Mutely she scoffed at her choice of words. Of the things she and Jackson might become as a result of this night, she'd already decided friendship could never be one of them.

"But you did make the call. A call I've waited..." Haley stopped short, only then admitting it was true. She had waited for his call, for the day he would need her. A startling admission she would need to give greater thought...but later, when his blue gaze didn't burn into hers, making anger and animosity meaningless.

Gathering scattered thoughts, she turned her attention to the cause of her journey. "I'm here for a purpose. Your horse needs attention. Now, Jackson, before it's too late."

"He'll be dangerous. Too dangerous."

"Because he's a fighter, yes, he will," Haley agreed. "But he's only restless now. Whatever this is, it's building. If I move quickly, hopefully I can find what I'm looking for. If I do and if my half-educated guess turns out to be lucky and right, what I'm trying might counteract it."

"'Educated guess'? 'Luck'?" It wasn't an admission he'd expected. He'd set his mind so strongly against her, he'd never considered what he should expect from her.

Pretending his touch and the softening of his demeanor didn't incite emotions she wasn't ready to deal with, Haley was determined to do the job she'd been summoned to do. Glancing at a clock visible beyond Jackson, she found this exchange that seemed to go on forever had, from beginning to now, spanned just nine minutes. Even that little time was too much. Too long.

Certain she was losing her window of opportunity, if there was one, she restated an inescapable truth. "You've never wanted me here. That you've called me tonight can only mean that you knew anything I might do was a last-ditch effort.

"Look at him, Jackson." Because she'd seen beyond the stubborn arrogance, because she'd felt the pain he guarded so carefully, she called his name softly. Hardly aware of what she did, with her free hand she touched his shoulder in compassion. "Time's running out, for Dancer and for me."

"No." Jackson couldn't explain why he was resisting this. He'd called for her help. When all else had failed, Dancer's survival rested, finally, in Haley Garrett's hands. The hands of a duchess, despite the calluses and blunt nails.

Over the telephone, it was a matter of course to consider that she should do this. But when she stood before him, so tiny and yet so determined, he realized how impossible it was that she face a half ton of maddened horseflesh.

"You can't. When I called, I didn't realize..." His voice drifted into silence. His hand tightened over hers, his shoulders lifted, as he made a choice consigning Dancer to certain death. "I'm sorry, Duchess. I shouldn't have interrupted the concert or your date with Daniel."

"It wasn't Daniel, and this is what I trained years to do. Why I relocated in Belle Terre and joined Lincoln's practice."

The exhausted stallion snuffled and took a stumbling step. Haley looked from Jackson to the horse and back. "Dancer isn't the first crazed creature I've confronted in my life and in my work. He won't be the last."

"Let her go, Jackson." Jesse spoke into the impasse. "I've seen your duchess in action. She can handle this *and* Dancer. Probably better than you or me."

As Jesse distracted him, Haley moved beyond Jackson's grasp. Syringe ready, she slipped through the stable door.

Two

Jackson Cade stood at the bedroom window. The bedroom he'd chosen as his when he'd bought the derelict farm the once-proud plantation had become. In debt up to his ears to the Bank of Belle Terre, he'd worked day and night, pouring his heart and his soul—and every spare penny—into the land.

When the effort seemed too much, his goal too impossible, it was this window and the view that kept him going. It was his measuring stick, the tally of his successes and his failures.

"How many times?" he wondered out loud. How many times had he stood here in dawn's light, watching the changes a day brought to the land. The changes his labor wrought as he reclaimed first one pasture then another. Acre by grueling acre.

Even with Lincoln and Jefferson helping, progress had been slow. More times than he could remember, he'd wanted to give it up. To count River Trace as Jackson Cade's folly. Then he would stand at this window at dawn. As his heart lifted with the sun, burdens seemed lighter, and impossible was only a word.

His first stud had been mediocre, not in keeping with the horse's own bloodlines, but its colts had had a way of reverting to an excellence that had gone before. A gamble, but there had been those willing to take the chance for that rare, splendid colt.

With the stud fees he'd added a second stud and another pasture, and his name became a whisper in all the right circles. Jackson Cade and Cade horses became a coveted secret. Then Adams sold Cade Enterprises, insisting a share of the absurd sum go to his brothers. They became silent legal partners, having no idea they *were* partners, whom Adams credited with being as responsible for the ridiculously simple invention a competing company fancied.

When the dust of the family battle settled, there were funds earmarked to set Belle Reve, the floundering family plantation, aright, and to keep it that way. Millions were left to be divided between brothers. Adams would have it no other way.

Gus Cade's sons, who had known nothing but hard work and penny-pinching times, were suddenly free of their beloved tyrant. And affluent into the bargain. But little had changed in their lives.

Adams stayed in the lowcountry and married Eden, the woman he'd loved forever. With her, he began rescuing the uninhabited and neglected houses of Belle Terre's infamous Fancy Row. Bringing grace and dignity to derelicts that a century before, in an accepted practice, grandly sheltered mistresses and second families of wealthy Southern planters and businessmen.

Lincoln brought his veterinary office and equipment to state-of-the-art, bought a Jaguar, a pied-à-terre on a secluded street in Belle Terre and left the rest for Adams to invest.

And Jeffie?

Jackson smiled as the name tumbled into his thoughts. Who knew about Jeffie? He still hunted, still fished, still painted. He worked with the horses at Belle Reve and River Trace.

And still had no idea the female population practically swooned at his feet.

A low laugh sounded in the pale darkness of Jackson's bedroom as first light gleamed beyond the window. A laugh of pleasure in his youngest brother. For, if all the rest of their lives had changed little, Jefferson's hadn't changed at all.

"Nor mine, truly." His life, his workload, his goals, were the same. Only River Trace had changed. Most of his own share of what he would always think of as Adams's millions had been poured into the farm. First replacing a barn that had burned. Arson, but with no motive discovered, nor any suspect.

Except the Rabbs, a local family waging a one-sided feud. An old enmity, sparked by jealousy of the Cades's misperceived wealth and anger over too many lost brawls. Jealousy and anger that turned to hate and danger and threatened tragedy.

With no proof and no more incidents, he'd filed his suspicions away. After the barn, he'd recouped and restored the last of the acres included in the original grant on which River Trace had been built. And, finally, the breeding stock. The studs, more and more costly studs.

Last came Cade's Irish Dancer. The stallion on which he'd gambled his dreams and the financial future of River Trace.

"I almost lost it," he muttered. "In a single night, I almost lost the dream."

As if it had lifted out of the east pasture, the sun climbed slowly into the sky, casting light over fields of grain waiting to be harvested. Miles of white fences gleaming like rose-gold ribbons traversed and intersected the velvet green of rich, grassy pastures. Horses snuffling dew-beaded grass were sleek and sassy, and so beautiful it hurt to watch them.

Paradise. Yes, for Jackson, the land he surveyed from his bedroom window was no less than that. Paradise lost, but for a tiny slip of a woman. A brave, savvy, fool-hearted woman, a woman he'd been determined to dislike from his first glimpse of her.

He'd rejected her help time and again. Yet when he called, she came. He insulted her, she kept her cool. He acted the boor—keeping her dignity, she made him the fool.

When all he had lay on the brink of destruction, with perception, compassion and ill-advised courage, at great cost to herself she had cared for a maddened creature and saved the day.

"No." He turned from the window to the bed where she slept, recovering from her near brush with death the previous night when a crazed Dancer had flung her violently against the wall of his stall. "She saved the night, my horse, and my home." Crossing to the chair where he'd spent all but the last few minutes keeping watch, he settled down to wait for Haley Garrett to awake.

The grandfather clock in the foyer had boomed the hour five times since Jackson Cade had put Haley in his bed. Four of those times she hadn't heard or stirred. On the fifth, she did.

Slowly, not quite awake, not quite asleep, her lashes fluttered but didn't lift from her cheeks. As the clock fell silent, a frown crossed her face, then was gone.

Six o'clock. She was late. She should be worried, but couldn't muster the energy. Not remembering the night, thinking only of the time, she stirred, beginning a languid stretch, and a sharp pain threatened to slice her in two.

"Oh-hh." An unfinished breath stopped in her lungs. Lashes that had just begun to rise from her cheeks at last, fluttered down in an effort to seal away a world too bright and an agony too sharp. She couldn't breathe, she couldn't move, as muscles across her back and midriff held her in paralytic misery.

Denying the pain, she tried to move again, and her teeth clenched a second too late to bite back a groan. A sound that brought with it the fleeting stroke of a hand across her brow. One offering comfort, but she didn't understand.

"No," she whispered hoarsely, and turned away.

"Shh. Everything's all right, thanks to you. You're all right," a voice assured.

Thanks to you. Thanks to you. She'd heard the routine before, trying to soothe what couldn't be soothed, undo what couldn't be undone, by planting a lie. God help her, she'd heard it all before and didn't want to hear it again. Keeping her eyes closed tightly, weary of an old struggle, she whispered, "Don't."

Haley was too tired. The words hurt too much. "Just don't." In the darkness of her world she shuddered as the bed dipped beneath his weight. "Go away, Todd. Leave me alone."

"Shh, shh. Easy," A deep voice, not the obsequious wheedle she expected. "I'm not Todd, Duchess. I don't think I'd like to be. But I won't touch you if you don't want me to."

The voice she'd heard soothing a frighten, crazed horse. Soothing her as gently.

"Jackson?" Gold-tipped lashes lifted. As she risked the turn to face him, eyes once as brilliant as a bluebird's wing were shadowed with more than physical hurt. Her gaze cleared, settling on his frowning features. As she remembered the night and the clock, deducing where she was, she checked a sharply drawn breath. Agony as sharp as the first crushed her ribs and spine in its vise.

Jackson watched her pallor grow more ghostly, and under his breath he cursed a man called Todd for sins he couldn't name, and himself for his own folly. "You're safe, Haley. And, because of you, so is Dancer."

"Dancer." The name fell from stiff lips as she remembered the stallion suffering the throes of madness. "He's alive?"

"Thanks to you. He'll need some time to recover, but eventually he should be good as new."

"How? When?" Haley was discovering there was a gap in her memory. The last she remembered was taking her hand from Jackson's and slipping into Dancer's stall.

"You guessed right on the cause of his symptoms. He was on the edge of another siege when you got the needle in him.

Whether it was the needle, the injection, or the cycle of the fits, Dancer sidestepped into you, pinning you against the stall wall.''

To Jackson's disgust, by the time he'd recognized Haley's intent, it was too late. Dancer had knocked her away as if she weighed nothing at all. She'd crumpled into a heap nearly beneath the horse's flying hooves before Jackson could get to her. The time it took to tear open the stall door so that he could shield her was the longest of his life.

"You have a bad bruise." Because he'd let her go. "And you'll be sore awhile." His fault, for calling her at all. "But Coop says you'll be right as rain in a week or so.''

"Coop? Cooper." She focused on the name, questioning and interpreting all at once. She heard nothing else Jackson said once she knew he was speaking of the dashing Davis Cooper, Belle Terre's physician and bachelor extraordinaire. Her escort for the concert. A friend who, over dinner, had subtly made her aware that he'd like more than friendship from her.

Abruptly, in her rush to answer the call to River Trace, she'd left him with barely an explanation or a backward glance. Not the way to treat a kind and gallant man. A would-be lover.

Haley struggled to sit up, unaware that in her cautious efforts the broad shoulder of the shirt she wore slipped down her arm. "I should have called him. I should explain." Not sure what Davis Cooper should know, or how she could begin to explain what she didn't understand herself, she abandoned the muddled thought. "I need to apologize.''

"For what, Duchess?" Jackson zeroed in on the little of the ramble he could decipher. "For doing your job? And doing it too zealously and too well?''

An understatement and a far cry from what he'd expected of her. No matter that she was Lincoln's associate, or that his brother would not choose a partner with lesser standards than he expected of himself. In his own stubborn mind-set Jackson knew he'd been unreasonable, believing only the worst of her.

"How I do my job isn't the point."

"Isn't it?" A questioning eyebrow inched up. A typical Jackson Cade reaction, usually accompanied by a teasing smile. But at the moment, with his conscience in turmoil, the typical Jackson Cade was having trouble finding anything to smile about. "Do you really believe that?"

"Of course I do. My work, underdone or excessive, isn't the point of the apology. Common courtesy is. Cooper behaved like a gentleman, the least I can be in return is considerate."

Touché, Jackson thought, though he knew there was no intended barb in the remark. He suspected she'd tolerantly filed away the memory of his behavior in the barn as one more Cade foible. If she remembered at all. Suddenly Jackson wasn't sure he liked being dismissed so easily. Even at his insufferable best.

Indifference. The passiveness of indifference was the last thing he expected from Haley Garrett. As she lay in his bed, with his shirt refusing to stay properly in place, he had no idea what he wanted. Or didn't want…except indifference.

"You can pay your dues to protocol later," he suggested after a pause in which his damnable shirt slipped another mesmerizing inch. "But…" He stopped, then continued his lecture. "I assure you an apology is neither due nor expected.

"Had the circumstances been reversed, don't fool yourself into thinking Coop would hesitate about leaving you. In the middle of a concert, in the middle of dinner, in the middle of…" His teeth clenched, briefly halting the outpouring. "Never mind about that one. What I'm saying is, that if a patient needs him, Coop's like a horse with blinders. Because he's so single-minded himself, he'll understand about last night."

Haley couldn't be so certain. "Maybe. If he knew the whole story, and how grave Dancer's situation had become."

"He knows, Haley. Coop was here last night." With a careful touch, Jackson leaned her back against a stack of pillows and adjusted the shirt. More for his own comfort than Haley's.

He was perturbed by what a glimpse of the curve of her bare shoulder had done to him. This was hardly the time or place for lust.

In any time or place, he reminded himself, the Duchess was all he'd schooled himself to dislike in a woman.

"Cooper's here? Now?"

With the repetition of Cooper's name, something altered in her face, even the shade of her eyes seemed to change. Jackson wasn't sure what it meant, and he discovered he didn't like it.

"It's morning." The paling sky had turned from red-gray to ever-changing blue. Light fell through ancient panes joining the dim glow of a single lamp. "Time all good little surgeons were at their operating tables."

"Morning?" She had forgotten the striking clock.

"It was morning before you finished in the barn. It's only a little later now." There were no roses in her cheeks, but like her perception, her color improved by the minute.

Turning her head carefully, Haley realized she was in a very masculine bedroom. Obviously Jackson's bedroom, not a guest bedroom. "That means I've been here for the remainder of the night?"

"What there was left after Cooper examined you."

"Cooper examined me?" As her mind cleared, she realized she sounded like a broken record. She laughed, and rued the impulse.

"Maybe you think Coop is deserving of an apology, but he would disagree. The way he sees it, he was an unchivalrous idiot to let you drive to River Trace alone. He arrived less than a minute after Dancer did his number on you."

"His number? On me?" Her back felt more as if a steamroller had flattened her, not a horse.

"He bucked, flinging you like a ball."

"You got me out." She didn't remember, but it wasn't a question. Jackson might dislike her, he might regard her veterinary skills and professional dedication as suspect, but he wouldn't stand idly by if she were in danger.

"With Jesse's help." Jackson spoke casually, leaving out every nuance of fear that had raced through him like cold fire.

He'd been wild when he'd thought she'd been crushed against the wall with all the brute's weight. Wilder when hooves that would have cut her fragile flesh to ribbons stomped over and over, narrowly missing her as she lay unconscious on the floor. Fear and galvanizing panic had given him strength he hadn't known he possessed. He didn't tell her that if Jesse hadn't kept a cooler head, calming Jackson as much as the horse, he would have killed Dancer with his bare hands. Nor that when she was safe, but he didn't know the extent of her injuries, he was a madman.

"Then Cooper came?" Haley frowned and pressed a massaging finger against her temple as she tried to make sense of the chain of events by putting them in proper sequence.

Jackson's head barely moved in a nod. "Cooper came."

Like a gift of fate, Cooper had arrived in the midst of the worst of Jackson's worry. And promptly threatened to eject him from his own barn, even forbidding him to watch, if he didn't stop hovering and cool down. Throughout the cursory examination conducted outside the stall, Jackson had paced. Impotent, helpless, a banished animal. After Cooper's determination that the bump on her head was simply a bump on the head, he continued with assurance that the breath had merely been knocked from her lungs when her back crashed into the wall.

Merely? Merely! Jackson had roared, adding angrily that he didn't see much damned difference, since Haley, by damn, certainly appeared to be unconscious. Unconscious and still. Frighteningly, heart-stoppingly still.

"He examined me?" Her eyes widened. If any trace of lethargy remained, the idea of being unaware and at the mercy of three men—three disparate men—brought it to a screeching end.

"You weren't exactly yourself." He saw confusion and chagrin in her face. It pleased him to see this coolly controlled and professionally confident woman falter. The pleasure was short-lived as the militant conscience of a gentleman, however reluctant, kicked in. "I doubt even Superwoman would be herself after being body-slammed by the stallion from hell."

"Body-slammed." Haley sighed and ignored the penalty the stupidity levied. Jackson painted a good description of the little she remembered. "Knocked the breath out of me, did he?"

Though she'd paled with the sigh, she tried to hide it behind a wry smile. After hours of watching her, Jackson had grown familiar with every nuance of her mobile features. He saw the pain but respected her efforts by making no comment beyond addressing her supposition. "Among Dancer's destructive behaviors, there was that. Along with a bump on the head.

"Which Coop assured me wasn't as much the reason you were lying in a puddle like a discarded doll as the breath thing." Anger kindled again as Jackson remembered how calm and controlled Cooper had been. As if a horse of River Trace causing injury to a beautiful woman were an everyday affair. "Which I told him was a damned fool thing to say. For, as far as I could see, unconscious was unconscious, no matter the cause."

After that cynical remark from Jackson, Coop had given her something to ease her enough that she would sleep. Then he'd launched into a detailed explanation, comparing Haley's condition with a child's tantrum, held breath and all. Before he could stop himself, Jackson had snapped back that in case Coop was too blind to notice, Haley wasn't exactly a child. And, in case Coop was too stupid to understand that tackling frenzied horses did not include holding one's breath, he ought to try one or both someday.

Cooper laughed then, with Jesse's guffaws joining in, while both watched him with smug, knowing looks. Which only made Jackson angrier, more frustrated. Which, he decided, excused him for being ornery. Explaining why Cooper's offer to take her to Jackson's bedroom—where, Coop pointedly reminded him, Jackson had insisted she rest and recover—was summarily dismissed. Which, to his mounting ire, produced another round of smiles.

It was the final straw when Cooper volunteered to stay. By then, finally convinced the Duchess was truly all right, and fed up with both Coop and Jesse, he nearly pushed each man out of the room. Then, gracelessly, he'd instructed Jesse to see to Dancer. With no more grace he suggested Cooper go home and wait for the next call, instead of dropping in.

Then he'd shut the door in their grinning faces.

"Why?" Jackson didn't realize he'd spoken the word out loud. The word he'd asked himself more times than he could count as he'd sat by her bed through the few hours left of the night. Why had he been so cavalier with Haley when, after all, he had called her? When her only sin, beyond interrupting a special evening to rush to River Trace, was wanting to help? Why had he been irritable with Cooper, whose arrival had been a godsend?

And Jesse? The man worked tirelessly, asking no quarter, giving none, as he fought for Dancer and with Dancer. Jackson knew his treatment of the old hand was unforgivable.

"Ask for help, then spit in the eye of any who do," he muttered, and turned from the bed and from Haley, to stare at the dawn that had become full-fledged morning.

"Is that what you call it?" Haley's voice was strained as she swung her legs over the side of the bed and rested her bare feet on the floor. Bare feet. She didn't want to think about that. Or that she was naked under the shirt she knew was Jackson's. Except for her panties. He'd left her that small shred of pride.

"Is that what I call—" Jackson had spun away from the window. In long, hurried steps he returned to her bedside. "What the devil do you think you're doing?"

"I don't think, Jackson. I know." Hands clutching the mattress, she tilted her head to meet his blazing gaze. "I'm getting out of your bed. And, if you'll bring my clothes, out of your shirt as well."

"You can't."

''No?'' The anger she'd conquered hours ago for the sake of a suffering animal flared now at the fierce arrogance. ''Watch me.''

The minute the words left her mouth, she knew her boast was worse than his bark. But pride wouldn't let her back down now. She knew something of her dilemma must have shown in her face when she felt his arms circling her, lifting her gingerly to her feet.

''Thank you,'' she murmured when she felt steady enough to speak. Glancing down at his muscular arms dusted with a pale auburn down, and conscious of his hands pressed against her back, strong fingers supporting, caressing, she whispered almost breathlessly, ''You can let me go now.''

''Of course.'' Jackson stepped back. His hands moved from her back to her shoulders, trailed down her arms, then curled over her clammy fingers. ''You're sure you can do this?''

''I'm sure. So long as I don't need to tackle another horse anytime soon, I'll be fine.''

Jackson laughed then, and released her. ''Yes, you will, won't you? Be fine, I mean.''

''It wasn't the first time…''

''I know,'' he interrupted softly. ''Nor the last.''

''I'm repeating myself.'' This time she didn't laugh.

''Doesn't matter.'' A gesture called her attention to a door opposite the hall. ''The bath's there. A nice hot soak should feel good about now. If you don't find all you need, just yell.''

''So long as the water's hot, I'll be fine.''

''Somehow I thought you would be. Since that's the case, I'll leave you to your bath, Duchess. In the meantime, I should be able to find some fresh clothes for you among Merrie's things.''

''Merrie?'' Haley knew she shouldn't be surprised there was a woman in Jackson's life. But she was. A dozen, maybe. No, not maybe, definitely. But not just one.

''Merrie Alexandre,'' Jackson explained. ''A university student who lived for a while with Eden and Adams. Between classes, and on weekends when she needs to escape her apartment mates, she helps here with the horses. Because she stays over when she works late, she keeps several changes of clothing here.''

Jackson let his gaze trail over Haley, lingering, remembering. But with none of the disdain of before. There wasn't much of her. but what there was, he'd discovered, was flawless.

Lastly, his gaze returned to her hair. The mane of pale gold Dancer knocked partially from the perfect coil, and he finished taking down, untangling it before putting her to bed. Even now he remembered the feel of strands like silk slipping through his fingers, the clean fragrance drifting from it. Enchanting. Enticing. Pale locks that would bind a man to her.

There were new tangles now, and his fingers curled as he thought of smoothing them again. Jackson rebuffed the thought and the path it was taking. Instead he moved to the bedroom door, opened it and stood with escape from his own awakening desire looming a step away. ''You're smaller, but I think I can find something that will serve. But don't worry, Merrie won't mind.''

Before she could even think to worry, Jackson stepped into the hall and shut the door. Haley was alone. ''Alone in the bedroom of Jackson Cade,'' she reminded herself as she wandered to the bathroom. ''It's just as well, considering that this show of kindness is contrition of the moment.

''Next week, this will be forgotten,'' Haley predicted as she turned on the taps, discarded Jackson's shirt and stepped into steaming water. ''Next week he'll hate me again.''

'''My apologies. Called away, but not for long. Dancer's fine, you needn't check him. Wait. Rest. I'll see you home.'''

Haley read out loud the note she'd found on the bed along with a selection of Merrie Alexandre's clothing. Crumpling the hastily scrawled missive, she let it fall to the floor along with the towel covering her from breasts to hips. Then she proceeded to dress, admiring the younger woman's taste, and disconcerted by Jackson's evident skill in making choices in women's clothing.

When she'd finished, she wondered briefly where her own clothes might be. Then, with a dismissive shrug, she counted them lost. Once the towel had been dropped in the clothes chute, her hair twisted into a helter-skelter knot and secured with what pins she could find, then the bed put in order, she was ready to go.

"Not one trace," she murmured. "He won't even remember I was here." Spying the note lying on the floor, she scooped it up and stuffed it into the pocket of the borrowed jeans. Making one last survey, pleased by the utter perfection she was leaving behind, she left it behind.

As she hurried to the barn, anxious to check on Dancer before the master of the house returned, Haley reflected that it felt good to be back in jeans and boots. And even the soft but sturdy blouse that tugged a bit too snugly across her breasts. Merrie was obviously slender, with a more adolescent figure. And, either she wore no bras, she'd taken all of that particular sort of garment back to her apartment, or Jackson had forgotten.

A breeze was just kicking up, in it lay the promise of rain. Nothing was prettier than a lowcountry rain falling like streaks of silver and gold as the sun would alternately hide or shine. Haley loved the autumn showers, and in anticipation she crossed the cobblestone path to the barn with a less guarded step. Her back still ached, but the soak and simply moving had eased it into a manageable state.

A draft skittered around the side of the barn, rattled the metal rings of rigging, and set a gate banging. The fabric of her shirt was supple enough to cling, sturdy enough to not be indecently revealing, and rough enough that with the movement of her body coupled with the efforts of the breeze, it brushed over the tips of her breasts, teasing her nipples to a pleasant tingle.

Haley's soft laugh at this secret pleasure was cut short by a low, deep bellow.

"What the hell are you doing here, and why the devil are you dressed like that?"

Spinning, she nearly collided with Jackson. As he glared down at her, she smiled with a calculated pleasantness, then sobered, assuming her most professional demeanor. "I'm here to check my patient. I'm dressed as I am because these are the clothes you chose for me."

"Then I made a mistake."

"Evidently you did. And, given your attitude, it's just as evident that before we're done with each other, it won't be your last mistake."

"What's that supposed to mean, Duchess?"

"You figure it out, Mr. Cade." Smiling another, equally calculated smile, she sauntered away.

"Who's Todd?" he called, expecting a reaction. Wanting one. Needing one.

His probing salvo produced nothing, not so much as a stumble in her step. With a dismissive waggle of her fingers, and maddeningly calm, she called back, "Todd's no one you need be concerned with. He's no one. No one at all, anymore."

Three

Five days. Five long, long days.

Frowning as he put the thought and its unacceptable implication out of his mind, Jackson flicked a glance at Jesse Lee. Beyond the usual half-mumbled good morning, each wrapped up in their own thoughts, their own chores, they'd spent most of the day barely speaking until they walked together to the west pasture. The pasture most visible from the entrance of the faded and tattered manor, where Dancer had been allowed his first day of true freedom. But only under the watchful eyes of guards strategically posted by Jericho Rivers, sheriff of Belle Terre and the surrounding county bearing the same name as the city.

It rankled, having armed men roaming the farm. The idea of strangers, regardless of how unobtrusive they were, tramping the land, disturbed and disrupted what had been a gratifying routine. But Jericho insisted. As a friend, as well as the local legal authority, he feared the crisis with Dancer was more than an isolated incident, and perhaps a resurgence of the vandalism that had burned Jackson's first new barn at River Trace to the ground. An unsolved crime that troubled Jericho. Now, as much as years ago.

Though he agreed with the need for the precautions, though he was more than grateful for Jericho's men, Jackson hated the atmosphere of an armed camp. He mourned the loss of the peaceful innocence that had settled over his land since the fire.

Peaceful or dangerously complacent? he wondered now, and was surprised. Complacency wasn't his nature. In fact, it was the last emotion he would ever be accused of harboring. Whatever he felt, right or wrong, he felt strongly. Obstinately.

"Yeah," he admitted under his breath. "Obstinate. Right, and especially wrong."

"You talkin' to yourself, boy?"

Jackson looked down at Jesse and shrugged. "Looks that way, doesn't it?"

"Well, I hope you're a mite friendlier to yourself than you've been to some other folks I could name."

"That bad, huh?"

"I'd say so."

"But you're still here. Why, Jesse?"

"Two reasons. First, you need me. Second, I figger your mad will pass, at least where I'm concerned."

"Have I thanked you? For what you did? For staying now?"

"No. But I 'spect you will. In time."

Jackson nodded silently and turned away. He owed Jesse far more than his thanks. The man was a walking encyclopedia on commonsense horse training and treatment. It was Jesse he'd called first. In the time following the stallion's strange malady, the cowhand had spent most of his waking hours at River Trace, calling on Jefferson for help, then leaving the stock at Belle Reve in his capable hands. Lounging now at Jackson's side, face shadowed by the hat brim tipped down against the late-afternoon glare, with his arms folded over the top rail of the fence, his keen regard never turned from the pasture.

"He looks good," Jackson ventured after a while.

"Yep." Jesse tracked the horse cantering across the pasture. "Friskier than a new colt." Slanting a sly assessing look at Jackson, he muttered half under his breath, "Which is more than I can say for you. Along with being grumpier than a junkyard dog looking for a leg to bite, you look like hell."

Warming to the subject, the older man studied Jackson's haggard features. "You know, for a man who just had his dream handed back to him by the prettiest little gal to come along in quite a spell, you don't look half as happy as I'd expect. Fact is, instead of being all smiles like any sensible human being should, lately you got more creases across your forehead left from frowning than this fence post has ridges."

Jackson bristled, proving Jesse's comment. "Let's see if I get your point, Jesse. Which am I, mean as a junkyard dog? Dumb as a post? A little of both? Or can't you decide?"

"Oh, I decided," Jesse responded mildly, refusing to be riled or distracted. "You helped me decide that sometime past. And by the way, you left out mule-headed." Before Jackson could bristle again, he patted a hard, broad shoulder. "What's the matter, boy? Not sleepin' so good these days?"

"I'm sleeping all I need to sleep." A mild exaggeration, but the sharpness eased out of Jackson's tone. Jesse was nosy, he pried, he meddled, he gossiped, but from the day he'd come to the lowcountry in answer to Jefferson's appeal for help, the best interests and well-being of the Cade family had become his first priority. Jefferson's younger years spent in Arizona working on the Rafter B for Jake Benedict had proven to be a godsend in many ways, Jesse Lee's loyalty not the least of them. In the balance, a little prying and meddling was a small cost to pay.

"All you need? Humph!" Jesse plucked a splinter from the rail, studied it closely, then flicked it away. "Don't appear so to me. In another week, what with the shadows lying under your eyes like blue hammocks and gettin' darker by the day, you're gonna look like the losing end of a bar hopper's brawl."

An innocent look wiped the worry from the cowhand's face. *Too* innocent, as he shrugged. ''Considering the extra security set in all the barns and around the pastures, by doggies, I can't rightly see what's keeping you awake.''

''We had security before. Not so tight, of course, but security. If I'm short of any sleep, I suppose it's because I keep remembering Dancer as he was then.'' Mild exaggeration had grown into bald lies. Or almost, by omission. For what Jackson couldn't get out of his mind was not just Dancer's screams, or even his critical condition.

No. What had him jerking from his dreams in a cold sweat was Haley Garrett. Like a tableau forever imprinted in both his waking and sleeping memory, the vision of that small, beautiful woman clinging to a frenzied brute of a horse played like a movie without end over and over in his mind.

He could still hear the sickening sound of her body striking wood. He saw flashing hooves flailing out in madness, falling ever nearer the unconscious woman. He still struggled to open a gate with fingers made clumsy with fear. And always there was the specter of being too late.

It was a nightmare that first sent him fleeing his bed, then left him sleepless, pacing and wrestling with yet another memory. The memory of undressing her, made too vivid by the night, a waking dream emblazoned forever on his mind by day.

Even now as his hands flexed within his gloves, the brush of soft leather became the brush of Haley's softer, naked flesh. He had only to close his eyes to remember her tawny skin burnished by the fall of lamplight, the fullness of her breasts with nipples dusky and barely furled like newly bloomed rosebuds.

In his more lucid times, he wondered why his memories confused him. From his first glimpse of her on the day she arrived in Belle Terre, a glimpse that sent every male hormone into feverish response and set every mental warning bell jangling, he knew she was trouble. Trouble with a capital T. Right then, right there, in the middle of Lincoln's office, he'd turned tail and bolted like a scared yearling. Then, as if escaping that first introduction wasn't enough, he held himself aloof, rebuffing every near meeting or close social encounter with a grim determination bordering on surly.

Surly, boorish, tactless, cruel. Hell, given his performance in the barn, he wasn't sure his vocabulary held enough words to describe his behavior.

And from the first, his efforts had been for naught. No matter how he avoided the woman of flesh and blood, in spirit Haley Garrett haunted him. No matter where he might go, or didn't go, at some time Lincoln's new partner would be mentioned.

At the local stockmen's meetings, at the inn, with his brothers, in his own blasted barns—at the feed-and-seed supply store, even the damned grocer's—as sure as breathing, her name tripped off someone's tongue. Then she would become the topic of conversation. And though he tried to not listen, he did. Like a man too long without water discovering a sweet, cool well, he drank in every word.

Each time he kicked himself afterward. Each time he denied he felt anything more than the fascination that goes hand in hand with aversion. Oh, he fought and struggled, he resisted and denied, and still the next time would be the same.

Haley wasn't a fool. She wasn't obtuse. Even the rare times he was subtle, she got the message. She knew how little he thought of her and her sort. If by some far-fetched chance she should misread him, he never let her forget. Even though he'd never been rude, crude, or anything less than a gentleman to any woman before. Ever. Lady Mary, his elderly, impoverished, and genteel instructor in deportment, had drummed Southern gentlemanly honor into each of Gus Cade's rowdy sons with astonishing success.

In all his years, Jackson had never strayed from that sweet lady's indelible instructions. Until Haley. Then there were no holds barred, no behavior too extreme. Even twinges of conscience weren't enough to dissuade him from his unreasonable vendetta.

He was unkind and cruelly mocking. Yet, when he'd needed her, she hadn't hesitated, or bristled, or backed down. Most of all, she'd refused to let him self-destruct by pushing her away one more time. Rather than exacting retribution for past mistakes, she'd pacified without groveling, and with dignity, called a truce. That small miracle accomplished, calmly and coolly competent, she'd done what she'd been called to do.

She'd saved his horse. But more than that, as Jesse pointedly reminded Jackson, she'd preserved the dream that had become his reason for living.

His antipathy for confident professional women was a learned response, based on one woman but applied to all for too many years for him to change. Yet only a fool wouldn't realize he should rethink the sweeping assessment. And Jackson had. At least in Haley's case. Though he wasn't changing, and only adjusting, the last insult had been hurled. The last skirmish fought. But he knew she would still haunt him. There could be no escape from his dreams of Haley Garrett, slender, fragile, almost perfect, buttoned chastely into his best silk shirt. His pillow would always carry the scent of his soaps and oils as altered by her body chemistry. No matter how pristine the linens, in his mind they would always shimmer with locks the color of captured sunlight.

Locks he'd drawn from their pins and combed with his fingers, wondering all the while how each shining strand would feel flowing over his body. And for just a little while, an impossible thought intruded. One he knew he couldn't allow, as he'd put her gently into his bed. Then, resolutely turning from her, he'd left her to sleep away the effect of Davis Cooper's sedative.

Once she'd left the farm, Jackson had thought to escape this malady—to ease the attraction. Now that he understood there was but one means of ease, and escape was impossible, his only recourse was to keep his perspective, control his male urges, and coexist.

Yes. That was the solution. Perhaps then, in keeping with another truce, Jackson Cade and Haley Garrett could be casual acquaintances. The sort of people who meet on the street and exchange meaningless pleasantries. No longer antagonists. Not quite friends.

And never, ever lovers! No matter that she set every male impulse raging within him like wildfire. But, if he went carefully, if he minded his P's and Q's as Lady Mary had taught him…ah, yes, they could coexist.

"…a tough time of it."

"What?" Drawn from his thoughts and pleased with his resolution, Jackson's temper flared at Jesse's observation. "What's tough about it? If I set my mind to it, I'll just do it."

Jesse's puzzled look questioned Jackson's immediate sanity. "Would you like to tell me what the dickens you're talking about? Or explain what it is you've set your mind to?"

Casting a wry smile at the cowhand, and stoking a hand over the taut muscles of his neck, Jackson shook his head. "Sorry, Jesse. I was thinking of something else. Nothing important."

Jesse's faded gaze narrowed. "Judging from your reaction just now, I'm not sure I would call it nothing important."

"But I did," Jackson reminded him. "So, since that's settled, would you like to repeat what you were saying?"

"Which part?" Jesse drawled.

"Which part? What does that mean?"

"It means I've been jawing at you for the last five minutes, and if you heard a word of it, I'll eat my hat."

Jackson laughed. His peace made with himself, his path set, his mood improved. "With or without salt and pepper?"

"Won't need neither one, will I?"

"No." A slow grin accompanied the admission.

"I don't reckon it would do a speck of good to speculate where your mind wandered off to," Jesse ventured.

"Don't reckon it would," Jackson agreed. "So why don't you run what you were saying by me again? At least the last part."

"Be glad to." Jesse's tone was just a little smug. "I was

saying Dancer's had a tough time. But he snapped back real quick-like. For sure, he's a handsome brute today, but I wouldn't a give a plugged nickel for him five days ago.''

There it was again. The count. Five days and fourteen hours ago, to be exact. To Jackson's mounting disquiet, like keeping score at a sporting event, keeping the hourly count had become the measure of his days, changing his nights.

First it was one day. Then two, next three and four. Now it was five days since Haley Garrett had answered his call, done what she considered no more and no less than her duty. Then, as if nothing extraordinary had occurred, she'd walked out of his life straight into his dreams.

Since the morning after, which was Jackson's true timetable, there had been no word from her. No interest in Dancer's progress. No anything. Probably because Davis Cooper was keeping her so busy. Coop made no secret that he'd like to add Haley to his list of conquests. ''Still,'' Jackson muttered sourly, ''busy or not, you'd think...''

Jesse cocked an eye at him and waited for the rest. Then his curiosity got the best of him. ''Well?''

''Well, what?''

''Well, what in tarnation were you going to say?'' With an emphatic finger, Jesse pushed his hat back a notch. ''That's what.''

Jackson shrugged and turned to lean on the fence as he watched the stallion prancing around a cattle egret that had landed at his feet. ''I was just thinking that it was strange that Haley—that Dr. Garrett hadn't called to check on Dancer.''

''What makes you think she ain't?''

Jackson turned to Jesse then. ''Has she?''

'''Course. Every day. Sometimes twice.''

''When?'' Jackson straightened from the fence. Standing a head taller, he glared down at Jesse. ''Why didn't you tell me?''

''Didn't think you'd care.'' Jesse lifted a shoulder, dismissing Jackson's irritation.

"Of course I care about Dancer." A fling of his hand gestured toward the pasture. "What else has all this been about?"

Jesse could have bristled back, for he was at River Trace only as a favor to Jackson. Instead, because he liked the third of Gus Cade's sons and suspected he understood the battle the younger man waged with himself, he answered quietly, "I know you care. Any tenderfoot could see how much. You'd never believe it in a hundred years, but you wear your heart right here." A light punch at a brawny arm underscored Jesse's point. "Clear as glass you are, Jackson Cade. For anyone who looks close."

"What the hell does that folderol mean?" Jackson was in no mood for Jesse's philosophizing. "And what does it have to do with the fact that no one told me Dr. Garrett called?"

"Dancer's fine. Better than fine. You don't like the little girl, so why would I upset you by talking about her?"

"She isn't a little girl, and what does liking her or not have to do with any of this?"

"Nothing, except I didn't think you were interested in anything about her," Jesse drawled. "Since it's clear I was wrong, you should know that next time she calls, we expect—"

"'We'? Meaning who?"

"The little girl and me."

"And you expect…?"

"The result of Dancer's pathology."

"Then she'll know what caused his seizure."

"Maybe." Jesse made a doubtful face.

"You don't think it can happen?"

"I think it won't matter." Jesse watched Dancer race across the pasture. "Mostly I figger we're lucky he's alive."

"You don't think it was just a prank. Maybe some fool kid sneaking into see what mischief he could stir up?"

Instead of answering, Jesse gave Jackson a long, considering look. Finally he sighed, muttering, "Do you?"

Jackson was thoughtful, as slow to respond. "No." His answer accompanied a grave tilt of his head. "No, I don't think it was a prank. It's what I'd like to believe. What I tried to believe, but it wouldn't wash. Not even for a second. Dancer represents millions of dollars on the hoof. But most important to me is that he's the making of a dynasty. What I truly believe is that someone out there knows what I have in him, and means to make certain it never happens.''

"Ain't likely the next try will be so easy. Now that the first failed and you're warned.'' Jesse's gaze locked with Jackson's. "There's one person you can thank for that.''

"Haley.'' Jackson said her name low and softly, unaware of what Jesse read into the quiet inflection.

"You've been so all-fired concerned that she hasn't called you, has it crossed your mind that it might be a good thing if you called her instead? Maybe apologize a little bit, and say thank you. Wouldn't hurt if you asked about her back. Bruises must be purpling up pretty bad about now.''

"You're right.'' He'd spent the better part of a week worrying about her. If he wasn't worrying, he was dreaming. Maybe it was good he hadn't spoken with her, or even knew she called. That negligence gave him the perfect excuse to see about her for himself. "But I'll do better than call, I'll go to her.''

"Just drop in? With no warning?''

"Sure.'' If he called, considering his past behavior, she'd likely tell him to take his concern straight to hell. If he just showed up on her doorstep, being the polite, reasonable little lady she was, she wouldn't turn him away.

"Jackson,'' Jesse called after him as he spun away from the fence, intent on choosing the proper attire for calling on a lady.

"No time, Jesse,'' he quipped over his shoulder. "I'm going into Belle Terre.''

"I don't think going without calling is a good idea.''

"You're wrong, Jesse. It's the best idea I've had in five days.'' Turning back briefly, he grinned and looked more like himself than in a long while. "No time to argue. See you later.''

Jesse watched him out of sight, lips quirking in concern.

"A damned fool thing to do. Showing up unannounced at a pretty lady's house might include discovering the rest of the male population of this lowcountry ain't as blind as Jackson Cade."

Pausing, squinting at the sun, judging the hour, suddenly Jesse chuckled. As Dancer veered toward the fence and stopped to nudge his shoulder, absently rubbing the horse's powerful neck, he chuckled again. "On second thought, maybe discovering the lady ain't so unpopular with the rest of Belle Terre's dandies is exactly what the young scalawag needs."

In response to the familiar voice and the soothing singsong tone, Dancer tossed his head and whinnied.

Jesse laughed out loud. "Exactly what I thought myself."

Jackson stood before the garden gate. He'd been there for five minutes. Ringing the bell of the town house that belonged to his brother Lincoln but was currently occupied by Haley Garrett should have been a simple act. Or so he thought. As it turned out, getting ready to eat crow wasn't any easier than deciding what to wear for that particular banquet. In the end, he'd chosen a pair of khakis and the dark green silk shirt he'd buttoned her into the night she'd slept in his bed.

At first he didn't understand his choice. Then he realized that subconsciously he was looking for an advantage. Maybe the memory of waking up wearing nothing but his shirt and her panties would make her just uncomfortable enough that she would agree to his proposition before she knew what hit her.

Yeah, that's what he thought, and for the duration of the trip from River Trace, his confidence soared. Now that the moment of first confrontation had arrived, he wasn't so sure. Hell, for the first time in his life, he wasn't sure of anything.

"Hey, mister," a young voice called. "You gonna ring that bell or not? You don't soon, your boo-kay will wilt."

Jackson turned, finding a small boy in tattered jeans and a

dirty shirt grinning a gap-toothed grin. A street urchin, whose
mother was likely one of the hookers who worked the wharf.

"It's okay. She won't bite ya. She's a nice lady." The urchin cocked an eye as black as coal at him. "You must be a
new one, ain't seen you around before."

"A new one?" Jackson asked.

"A new fella." Moving to the gutter, the boy jerked up a
rusted bike and mounted it. "I was going to ask if I could do
some chores for her, but since she's 'specting company, I'll
wait."

Before Jackson could ask another question, the boy was
wheeling across the street, weaving in and out of sparse traffic
like a pro. A rare horn blared, almost drowning out the call
that floated back to him. "Just ring the bell, mister."

Jackson rang the bell.

"Hi. You're early," her voice sounded over the intercom.
"But that's okay. Come on in, the gate's open. If you like,
you can have a glass of wine in the garden while I finish
dinner."

He pushed open the gate. Familiar with the layout from the
days Lincoln used it as his pied-à-terre, Jackson needed no
more instructions. Wondering why Jesse had taken it upon
himself to call and warn her, he strolled down the walk,
climbed the steps, and stopped at the door.

"'Just ring the bell, mister,'" he quoted the urchin, and
pressed his thumb against another small, lighted circle. While
he waited, he looked out over the garden. It hadn't changed
since he was here last. A little overgrown because of her injury, maybe. But nothing an hour or so with a pair of clippers
couldn't remedy.

He was standing with his back to the door when it opened.

"Hello?" He heard the question in her voice. When he
turned, he saw surprise in her face. "Jackson?" Catching a
quick breath, she amended, "I mean, Mr. Cade."

"You were expecting someone else?"

"Ah." She licked her lips as if her mouth had suddenly
gone dry. "Well, yes, I was."

Jackson felt like a fool standing there with a garden filled with flowers at his back and a bouquet clutched in his hand. Jesse hadn't called. Haley had thought he was one of the "fellas" the street urchin had spoken of. "I'm sorry." He felt the heat in his face. "I shouldn't have come without calling. I didn't think…" He was floundering, making things worse. "It's Friday, I should have realized you would have a date.

"I'll leave before he arrives." He was already striding down the walk, eager to be away, with the bouquet still clutched in his hand. "Next time I'll call first."

"Jackson." Her voice was gentle, without a trace of anger or ridicule. "Don't go."

He considered, then refused. "This was a bad idea."

"Please stay."

He turned back. Nothing in the world could have kept him from turning back to her. He wanted to see her face, to hear her say his name again in that gentle way. "I won't be intruding?"

"Of course not."

She stepped through the door and waited on the veranda. Her dress was silvered gold, like her hair. He was inordinately pleased to see that whoever her date was, she hadn't worn it down for him. Inordinately pleased until he remembered how seductive taking away each pin, then watching glittering strand stumble to her shoulders like a sunstruck waterfall, had been.

"You could join us for dinner. Yancey wouldn't mind."

"Yancey!" The crush of his grip threatened to break the stems of the bouquet. "Yancey Hamilton?"

Haley laughed, the column of her throat moving delicately with the sound. "There's more than one Yancey in Belle Terre?"

"I hope not. I mean, one's enough." Good grief, and he'd worried about Davis Cooper.

Her laughter turned to a frown. "You don't like Yancey? I thought he and all the Cades were best of friends."

"We were. I mean we are." But friendship didn't blind Jackson to Yancey's faults, or to his unconscious prowess in collecting women. Lord, they loved him, had always loved him. Even now, when he roared into town on his big black motorcycle, wearing boots and jeans and a leather jacket, with his black hair barely dusted with silver dipping over his forehead, no one was immune. The word *no* seemed to vanish from the feminine vocabulary.

He had one saving grace. No, two. And, conversely, both made him even more irresistible. First, Yancey, ever the bad boy of Belle Terre, was truly a gentleman. Second, beyond a little flattery and flirting, but for the rarer than rare mutual dalliance, *he* was immune.

But would he be to Haley? Somehow, Jackson didn't think so. "All right," he heard himself saying. "If you truly don't mind, I'll stay."

"I don't mind, Jackson. If I minded, I wouldn't have asked. Make yourself comfortable, have a glass of wine. I'll set another place at the table, then we'll talk until Yancey arrives."

With a tilt of her head, in that subtle way she had of negating the differences in their height, her gaze met and held his. "That is why you came, isn't it? To talk?"

"Yes."

"And these are for me?" In a three-fingered caress she stroked the pale petals of the gardenias.

Fascinated by her composure, Jackson only nodded.

"Why?" Blunt but gentle. With her eyes and mouth unsmiling, she asked, then waited.

"A peace offering." There was nothing else he could say. Nothing he could add. His words, needing no frills to dress them up.

It was his turn to wait while her solemn gaze moved over his face, lingered on his mouth as if she could read unspoken truths there, then returned to hold his gaze in a clear, unwavering regard.

After a time that might have been two seconds or two minutes, she took a long, not-quite-steady breath. Reaching out with both hands, she took his flowers and brought them to her face, touching her cheek with their petals.

Haley looked up, eyes as blue as the sea as it meets the sky, touching him. Then she smiled her beautiful smile as she whispered softly, "Yes."

A truce, granted with one word.

After all he'd said and done.

Four

"Come in, Jackson. Please."

She led him inside graciously, as if he appeared on her doorstep everyday. For an uncertain moment he stood inside the foyer, observing the changes she'd made in Lincoln's small house. Changes adding modern comforts with a tasteful, feminine touch. A reflection of a calm, composed personality, even as every alteration remained true to historic Belle Terre style.

A book lay open and facedown on the small sofa as if she'd been reading it. Unabashed curiosity enticed him to it. With his fingertips he traced the title emblazoned across the slick jacket. "'Chiaroscuro,'" he read quietly, paused thoughtfully, then read the subtitle. "'Lights and Shadows in Old Belle Terre.'"

She laughed again, a sound that filled the tiny room with music. "Less than two minutes inside my home and you've discovered one of my secret passions."

"Four," he corrected. Still bewildered by her welcome, but

warmed by her laughter, his tongue seemed to have a mind of its own as the words flowed easily. "That you read. That you like old houses and gardens. And my brother Adams' book."

There were more secrets Jackson would like to discover about Haley Garrett. Passions he would know—if this were more than a superficial association held intact by imaginary accord.

She came to stand by him, her perfume drifted around him. A subtle, delicate scent that reminded him of sunlight after rain. As she marked her place and closed the book before laying it aside, her arm brushed his shirt. Jackson looked down at her, wondering if she remembered that she'd worn it, and where.

If she remembered, the memory didn't disturb her, for when she looked at him, her eyes were clear and, as always, calm. "I've enjoyed the book and put it to use. Lincoln suggested it when he discovered I was fearful that in redecorating the house I might do something to spoil it. He assured me I could do whatever I wished. But as a tenant, I couldn't bring myself to make any changes without some background knowledge.

"It's a lovely old house." There was both love and respect in her tone as her gaze left his, touching on surviving historical details that made homes such as Lincoln's unique. "Too lovely to be spoiled by ignorant mistakes."

Dismissing the subject, embarrassed by her fervor, she turned to a narrow sideboard. Taking up an open bottle of wine, she filled two antique flutes and returned to him.

With a graceful gesture, she invited Jackson to take a seat on the sofa. When she'd joined him, her fragrance once again tantalizing him, she commented, "Adams is quite good in describing and explaining the style and architecture of these old Southern homes. He writes with a fondness as well as a wonderfully descriptive style. Sometimes I feel as if I were actually walking through the rooms he speaks of.

"He paints pictures in words of black and white as skillfully as Jefferson does with oils and canvas. Until I read his book, I never realized that chiaroscuro and its fascinating aura contributed so much to the appearance of the city and its houses. More than understanding it, Adams made me *see* it.''

Jackson settled back on the sofa, sipping the wine, a piquant Merlot. Without knowing her, without letting himself know her, he'd dismissed her as the typical, hard-edged, single-minded career woman, with no concerns beyond her ambition. Now, with each passing moment, he discovered Haley Garrett was a multifaceted woman with many talents and myriad interests.

He watched her over the rim of his glass. Of course she was well traveled. Which made him wonder, as he had too many times when she wandered unexpectedly into his thoughts, what had attracted her to Belle Terre. Quaint, lovely, and genteel though it was, what did such a small, charmingly pompous, Southern city have to offer her? What was so alluring that she'd walked away from whatever her life had been, bringing little but herself and her skills?

At first he'd suspected it was Lincoln who had drawn her here. More than once, he'd wondered if she were in love with his second oldest brother. Then, in a rare moment of common sense concerning her, he realized how foolish the thought was. If Haley wanted Lincoln, why wait until he was happily married to make her move?

He couldn't comprehend her values. He would be the first to admit that now. But anyone with a brain wouldn't need to comprehend to know that intruding in a marriage wasn't her style.

She was...what? he wondered. Thirty-one? Thirty-two? Lincoln had only said she was younger than he. A whiz kid, a product of a number of outstanding European schools. Some of them private, very elite, catering to the super intelligent. In *his* short escape from Gus and adding to his degree in forestry, Lincoln had gone only a year late to a school of veterinary medicine in California. Haley had been younger, but a classmate.

How much younger? Jackson allowed himself the luxury of looking at her, really looking, as he hadn't before except as he'd watched her sleep five days ago. And in his misbehaving dreams. In certain lights she looked like a mature teenager. One of those modern, hot little chicks who had it all together, who knew who she was and, definitely, what she had.

Then she would speak, or move, or smile, and no one could doubt that she was a mature, accomplished woman. And beautiful.

No, beautiful wasn't the word. Arresting. She had only to step into a room and conversations would pause, heads turn. He'd seen it. Like a wave washing over the shore, an awareness that Haley Garrett had arrived would flow through a gathering.

Did she know? To his surprise, he'd begun to suspect she didn't. Even that she wouldn't believe it if he should tell her.

But he wouldn't tell her. Just as he wouldn't tell her how fetching she'd been in her little black dress with the sexy slit revealing far too much of one shapely leg. A sexy dress, leather gloves, scuffed and worn boots, and a share of courage bigger than she that had nearly driven him mad.

No matter that Jesse was watching, no matter that Dancer was screaming and wild and he was just as wild with worry— one look and he wanted to take her in his arms. Wanted to hold her, kiss her, to lie with her in a bed of hay and make love to her.

Dear God. He'd wanted her.

For weeks—no, months—he'd worked at disliking her. Struggling to hold on to a long-standing prejudice. One that had shaped his young life and hardened into conviction with time. Unreasonable? Perhaps. But at this late date it was impossible to change. Truth: he didn't want to change.

In fact he was determined he wouldn't alter his opinion one iota. Then, just when he thought he'd succeeded, that his conviction was hardened beyond doubt, she'd walked into his barn. And all his struggle had accomplished had been swept away. If not for Jesse and Dancer, he could have made a fool of himself then and there. Later, in his bedroom, if not for her pain and the oblivion induced by Cooper's powerful sedative, he would have.

He might have been half-crazed by desire strong enough to melt old walls like snow in a lowcountry July, but he'd had five equally maddening days of battling memories and grimly trying to stave off dreams. Both had been enough to kindle his stubborn streak. Which meant that each day of resurrecting those walls had lent new strength to his determined resistance.

Though he'd come with an altered opinion, and even in respect, he was offering tenuous friendship. No less. Never more.

"Jackson?" The sound of his name as only she said it roused him from his reverie. "Is something wrong?".

"Nothing's wrong." Realizing he'd been staring at her—blatantly—assuming a nonchalance he didn't feel, he turned the burden of explanations back to her. "Why do you ask?"

"You were staring at me." For the first time she seemed ill at ease. "And you were frowning as if you were angry."

"I'm not angry, Haley. And certainly not at you."

"Oh," she said, accepting his answer but still puzzled.

Jackson waited, but she said no more. He was discovering she had that rare capacity of being still and silent in tense situations when most babbled in disquiet.

Beyond the open door a hummingbird chittered, drawing his attention. Then the tiny creature was silent as it sipped from a flower, leaving only the stir of leaves and the splash of the fountain to resound through the walled courtyard. With the heat of summer diminishing as the season slipped into barely less temperate days of autumn, the garden was lush with foliage layered in shades of green. Its colors all the richer in contrast to dappled patches of fading sunlight and deepening violet shadows.

"Light and shadow." Jackson returned his attention and his thoughts to Haley. "At times a source of beauty."

Haley nodded, sharing his thoughts. "Chiaroscuro."

"You speak the language?" He phrased it as a question but

he heard his answer in the way she spoke the word. The perfect inflection, the deeper understanding.

"Italian?" The smile was there again, this time a little self-deprecating. "Some. At least enough to recognize the word. I lived in Italy, briefly. Very briefly, when I was a young girl."

"One of your father's assignments?" Among the little he'd allowed himself to discover about her, he'd learned that most of her father's duties involved the diplomatic corps. Italy wouldn't have been a far-fetched possibility.

"Actually, it was where my mother chose to live when my father was assigned to an embassy in a country where she couldn't go. I was too young to understand why."

"Did that happen often?"

"No, at least not where my mother was concerned." Haley turned her glass, watching the ruby liquid catching glancing rays cast by the lowering sun. "There were more times when my parents felt the location wasn't suitable for my brother or me."

"Your brother?" No one, not even Lincoln, had ever mentioned she had a brother.

"Sammy." Haley lips tilted as if thoughts of her brother were a mix of pleasure and another emotion he couldn't fathom. "Except now that he's older, only his family still calls him Sammy, and then only on forgetful occasions. To the rest of the world, he's Samuel Ethan Garrett. Or just Ethan."

"Ethan Garrett. The expert on oil well fires?"

"Among other things that go bump in the night, or the day. He loves danger and challenge. Any challenge. Anywhere." The explanation served as her answer. The flute turned. Wine splashed against the glass, betraying the tremor in her hand.

"We worry," she added. "Sammy...no, *Ethan*." A frown was quickly banished as she corrected her error. "Ethan thrives."

"Where is he now?" Jackson set his half-filled glass aside, too intent on Haley and her veiled distress to drink the wine. "Or do you know?"

"He goes where he's needed, for as long as he's needed.

Our parents and I usually hear where he's been, rather than where he is, or where he's going.'' Before he could ask, she explained. ''My father's assigned to the Pentagon. My parents live in Virginia.'' She named an area not far from the nation's capital, and famous for great horse farms. ''I lived nearby before coming to Belle Terre.''

''Why *did* you come to Belle Terre, Haley?''

Sighing, she set her glass aside. ''A number of reasons. One was to work with Lincoln. You must know he's one of the most brilliant men in our field.''

Jackson inclined his head in agreement. ''I know.'' Without missing a beat he asked, ''And the other reasons?''

''I wanted a home. A real home in a peaceful area. Of all the places I'd lived, Belle Terre was my favorite.''

That took Jackson by surprise. He had no memory of a younger Haley Garrett living in Belle Terre. Surely their paths would have crossed somewhere, at some time. At Belle Terre Academy, in Lady Mary's deportment classes. At some of the social functions. One thing was certain, she wouldn't have been a girl he could have forgotten. At least he didn't think so.

''Good heavens!'' Haley exclaimed, bringing an uncomfortable subject to a close. ''You came to talk, and so far I've done all the talking.'' Rising from her seat but gesturing, a second too late, that he shouldn't rise, too, she had to tilt her head to look up at him. ''I should check on dinner. Have another glass of wine, and when I come back, it's your turn.''

Jackson remained standing as she left the room. Almost an escape, as if he'd touched on a subject she didn't want to discuss. But what? Her brother? Where she'd lived before? Why she'd left and why she'd chosen Belle Terre?

The ordinary subjects between new acquaintances. Innocuous subjects. Or were they?

Puzzled, he watched her—the way she moved, how the long, pleated skirt clung to her narrow hips, then flared and swirled just above her ankles. Her blouse was a close fit, skimming over her breasts before narrowing into a banded neckline that emphasized the graceful column of her throat. Her shoulders and arms were bare, but there would be no bruises there to hide.

And no scars.

The scars were more intimately and cruelly placed. Jackson remembered the horror of each as clearly as if he could see them now. Five livid circles arranged like the petals of an obscene flower below her left hipbone. They'd been barely visible above the slipping elastic of the panties she'd worn the night she'd come to River Trace. But once glimpsed, no one could ever forget.

Five scars. Obvious cigarette burns, puckered and white against the backdrop of healthy, tawny flesh. A sacrilege. The despicable desecration of a body so beautiful. Of any body.

He knew beyond question no accident had caused them. He only wondered if they were part of her reasons for moving to Belle Terre. A brand, manmade by some cruel, sadistic...

Jackson heard the snap of the stem of his glass and felt the prick of a broken shard before he felt the blood. It was only a sliver, easily removed, blood quickly checked. No harm done. No sacrilege committed as by one of Haley's crazed creatures.

"Jackson?" Haley stood in the doorway leading from the kitchen, holding his gardenias in a blue vase. "Is something wrong?"

"Only that like a clumsy oaf, I broke one of your glasses. There are some of the same sort at River Trace. I'll replace it."

"Are you hurt?" Before he could assure her, she had set the vase aside, crossed the room, and was taking his hand in hers. Her touch was cautious, her fingers cradling his were soft and calloused. An intriguing mix. But never as intriguing as the woman.

"I'm sorry," she apologized. "The glass was old and too fragile to use. But it was so pretty. "Now look what I've done."

She lifted a heart-stopping gaze to his. In it he saw the

compassion she felt for all wounded creatures. Even a bastard such as he. Jackson knew then that if the man who had hurt her, literally branding her, ever touched her again, he would kill him.

He didn't know how he knew it was man, but he knew.

"It's nothing, Duchess. I've had worse from a splintering fence rail." *Duchess.* The name, *his* name for her, begun as an insult, sounded more and more like an endearment.

Suddenly he knew he should leave. Coming to her had been a mistake. A friendly truce was impossible. "I should go. I've interrupted your evening." Taking back his hand, he hurried away. He was poised at the door when she stopped him.

"You came to talk, Jackson. Talk now, before you leave."

He heard the strength in her voice. But didn't compassion and caring such as Haley's normally come from great strength?

"It was nothing. Just an apology." His lashes shielded his eyes. He couldn't bear to see her rejection of his bumblings.

"Thank you," she said simply, taking his words at more than face value. Not turning the other cheek, or exacting retribution by demanding more, just accepting.

"That's it?" His eyes snapped open, then narrowed. "That's all you want from me? All you expect?"

"What right do I have to expect more, Jackson? Much of what we feel is based on instinct, not conscious thought. It isn't completely in our power to decide which person we will like and which we won't. Since we both live here, and obviously our paths will continue to cross, I'd hoped that if ever you got to know me, you might like me at least a little better.

"Failing that, I hoped I could earn your respect for my work, if not for myself. That you're here now, making an effort that must be difficult, gives me hope that I've managed to succeed in the latter. I'd wished for more." Her smile was rueful, but resigned. "Even so, I'm grateful for this. For today."

"Grateful!" God help him, she was going to destroy every defense he had. He'd feared he would see hatred in her eyes.

Now he knew it would be easier if he had. How did one resist kindness and compassion, and common sense? How did he resist *her*?

"My attitude has less to do with you than with me." A bold, uncommon admission for the hothead. "It was just... Ah, damn, Duchess." Struggling, he looked away. Jesse was right. He did wear his feelings on his sleeve, and too often a chip on his shoulder. The rationale for the latter he kept buried deeply, for it was too painful to explain. He settled for a half-truth. "I'm not sure I understand myself."

He gripped the jamb of the open door. The scent of gardenias drifted from the garden, blending with his. The broken wineglass, lying as he'd left it on the table, looked no more shattered than Haley.

He'd come offering peace. She'd taken it a step further, offering unquestioning absolution for unforgivable offenses. He had to wonder why. Why hadn't she just written him off as an insufferable imbecile? What did she see in him that merited even the smallest kindness?

Haley was neither a fool nor weak. She wouldn't subscribe to the theory of masculine superiority for as long as a heartbeat. What she'd offered came from the heart, as an equal.

Understanding her strength and believing in her kindness did not answer his dilemma of why? Why would a woman who had so much to offer the world and the right man trouble herself for even a minute over a flaming son of a bitch?

The epithet rankled, but it was true.

An unbearable truth.

Haley stood as he'd left her. She wasn't a woman to pry. Harboring secrets of her own, he knew she would respect his. Yet he couldn't leave her without an explanation, no matter how lame.

"Haley." He wondered how he could say what he must. Then realized there was but one way with this woman. The truth, no frills. "Just understand that it's me—all of it, every moronic word, every unconscionable insult. Me, not you. For what it's worth, I respect you and your work. I've never known a woman with your courage and compassion. I doubt I ever will again.''

She didn't smile, but he saw the shine of pleasure in her eyes. As her gaze held his, he wanted to take her into his arms. To kiss her soft lips and stroke her body, seeking out the secret places, awakening a need for a different, greater pleasure. He wanted her gentle hands touching him, he wanted her kiss.

He wanted Haley Garrett. He understood that now. But he couldn't have her, for he could never be sure he wouldn't hurt her again. With the indelible memory of five ugly scars burned into his mind, he knew she'd been hurt too much already.

For the sins of another man, and for his own, he would never know what it was like to make love to the only woman who had ever torn away his defenses and touched his heart.

He didn't love her. Not yet. Love needed care, it needed to be cherished, it needed honor. Emotions he hadn't allowed in his judgment of her. And unlike desire and lust, without them, love would wither.

No, he didn't love her, yet it hurt to leave her. But he knew he should before he made a worse mistake than he had already.

''I owe you more than I can ever say.'' He heard his own voice. He heard words he hadn't meant to say. ''But we can't be friends. Surely you know that, Duchess.''

She didn't move, or breathe, as he watched the light go out of her eyes. But her head tilted just a fraction. Only the little needed that he saw the depth of her pride, the power of her courage. ''No, Jackson, I don't know. I don't understand. But I'll try.''

The shine was back in her eyes. This time, the sheen of tears. Proving his point, driving it home, he'd hurt her already.

''I won't avoid you, Jackson, and I won't run from you,'' she promised. ''But I'll try to see that our paths never cross.''

He nodded, knowing he would do the same. But he couldn't leave it at that. ''If there's trouble…if you need me for any reason, call me. Just whistle—'' he tried for a smile that didn't work ''—and I'll be there. Anytime, any place.''

"Thank you." Her posture didn't relax. "But I could never ask you for help, Jackson. You've done enough already."

He looked for sarcasm. There was none. She meant exactly what she said. Jackson turned back to the door, wondering what in hell he'd ever done for Haley Garrett except…damn his black heart! He didn't want to think about what he'd done.

Keeping his back to her, his hands braced again against the doorjamb as if for support, he stopped. "I'm sorry, Duchess. I wish it could be different."

Her voice was a ragged whisper. "So do I, Jackson."

Then he was out the door, across the veranda, and down the steps. Twilight had deepened and hovered on the brink of nightfall, but Jackson didn't see. A void deeper and darker than any night lay where his heart had once been. He'd hurt her intentionally. Then, realizing what a fool he'd been, he'd come to make amends and hurt her again.

He'd been who he was and what he was for too long to change. He knew it, and by now Haley knew it, too. Too well to ever want him, or need him, or find pleasure in his touch.

His footsteps sounded hollowly on the stone path, his head was down. He had no idea he wasn't alone until a pair of strong hands clasped both his shoulders.

"Whoa, Jackson. Where's the fire?"

"Yancey. What are you doing here?" Then he remembered Haley's dinner engagement.

"The same thing you are, I imagine, visiting the prettiest lady in Belle Terre." In the flicker of gaslights, Yancey's calm eyes watched him, even as his handsome mouth tilted in a rakish smile. "Considering your sisters-in-law, maybe I should amend that to the prettiest, *single* lady in Belle Terre."

"Yeah," Jackson grumbled. "Maybe you'd better."

"Well, now." The Southern drawl Yancey slipped in and out of at will grew more pronounced. "Who stole your candy?"

"Don't be ridiculous. Nobody stole anything."

"Maybe not." Yancey's keen green gaze studied his friend's face. "But something sure put you out of sorts." The taller man's hand's dropped from Jackson's shoulders as he backed up a step. Glancing toward the veranda, he saw Haley. Her face, caught in the light spilling from the house, was tense and pale. "You haven't been quarreling with Haley, have you?"

"We haven't been quarreling," Jackson muttered.

Yancey looked from one to the other. Neither looked too happy. "As I recall, you two haven't exactly been friendly. So, suppose you tell me why you're here in the first place. And why you're practically running away, in the second."

"I'm not running," Jackson snapped, the famous temper of the third son igniting. "To repeat so it sinks into your thick skull, Yancey Hamilton, maybe we haven't been friendly, but we haven't been quarreling."

Catching a heated breath, Jackson launched deeper into his response. "Not that it's any of your blasted business, I came to thank Haley, and to make peace."

"Hmm," Yancey drawled. "If this is peace, you're going to be hell in a lovers' quarrel"

"This isn't a lovers' quarrel," Jackson snapped.

Yancey grinned. "Coulda fooled me."

"Ah, hell, Yancey," Jackson growled. "Haley did me a favor. I was an ass. I came to apologize. That's it."

"Mmm-hmm."

"Quit saying that." In a wild gesture, he waved toward the house. "Go eat your dinner before it gets cold."

Yancey laughed softly. "Oh, I'm not worried, Jackson. Not in the least. Haley's a great one for warming things up."

"She...what?"

"I said Haley's a great one for—"

"Never mind," Jackson cut him off. "I heard you."

Yancey laughed again. "Then, if you're sure you're leaving, I'll say good night."

"Yeah. Good night."

Long and lean and dark, with silver streaks in his hair catching the lamplight, Yancey moved down the walkway to Haley, who waited on the veranda.

"Yancey." The name drifted out of flickering darkness.

"Yes?" Yancey turned and stepped closer because Jackson spoke softly.

"I don't know what's between you. It isn't my business. But don't hurt her. She'd been hurt too much already."

"I know," Yancey said simply, grimly. "The last thing I would ever do is hurt Haley."

Jackson stood for a moment, wondering what it was Belle Terre's bad boy knew. When Yancey said no more, Jackson, feeling like a fool standing in the garden keeping two friends, perhaps two lovers, from their dinner, turned away.

Yancey watched him a second longer, then turned again and moved quickly to the veranda.

"Yancey?" Haley moved to him. "Is there news of Ethan?"

"Yeah, sweetheart, there is," Yancey said in an aching whisper. "I'm afraid it isn't good."

At the open gate, Jackson looked back over the garden and the veranda. He saw Yancey take Haley into his arms.

For as long as he could bear to watch, he did. Then wearily he stepped through the gate, closed it with a sad finality, and walked away.

Five

Haley folded the jeans, then the shirt, and laid them aside. Both had been carefully laundered, neatly pressed, and set aside for more than a week. Each time she was drawn to them in indecision, she found herself unfolding and refolding them.

Merrie Alexandre's clothing, clothing she'd worn after her own had been ruined at River Trace. Even though Jackson assured her Merrie had other changes at the farm, there was still no good excuse for having kept these for so long.

Haley had no idea where Merrie lived, and there was no number listed for her in the phone book. Eden, of course, could easily have solved the dilemma. Given Adams's wife's warm, generous nature, she would likely have gladly assumed the responsibility of returning the borrowed garments.

"So would Lincoln, now that he's back home on the farm." Rising from her bed, crossing to the open French doors, Haley looked out at the city. Lincoln had returned from his seminar and combined vacation, then promptly insisted she take a day off. To rest, he'd said, from bearing the brunt of managing the practice alone for nearly two weeks.

A lie, but a kind one. In the months she'd been in the low-country, she'd managed the practice alone before. For a number of weeks, in fact, when Linsey Stuart and her young son, Cade, had arrived to take up residence on the Stuart farm, turning the ever-calm, pragmatic Lincoln's life upside down.

Now it was Haley's life that was in turmoil. It hadn't taken long to learn that managing the practice alone was more difficult when she spent most of her nights lying sleepless from worrying about two men. Ethan and Jackson.

Though she demurred at the offer of a day off, she'd welcomed a quiet time. But only at first. It hadn't taken long to realize a day away from her busy routine was a mistake. Quiet time alone was not the solution. And rest? Impossible. She needed busy hands and a busier mind to keep the preoccupations of the restless darkness of her nights from becoming total obsession in idle daylight.

"Two," she muttered, and smoothed a palm over her forehead and down the length of the braid lying over her shoulder. Two men who meant more to her and drove her closer to the brink of furious distraction than any other in the world. Ever.

Two very different men. Both of whom Yancey had discussed over dinner and after, just days before. Thus the greater unsettling of her life, and her dreams.

The first and most crucial—Ethan—he'd spoken of woefully briefly. The second he'd discussed at length, reminiscing throughout the evening. In part to distract her from concerns she couldn't change. But also to give her some insight and a new perspective on both the city and county of Belle Terre, and its most puzzling citizen.

But, however brief the first, at least it meant information and even word from her brother. Which was infinitely better than the unknowing silence after Yancey's mysterious contacts first learned from other mysterious sources that Ethan was wandering some South American jungle. That he was keeping one step ahead of the drug cartel that wanted his head on a platter.

The single message her brother finally managed to get directly into Yancey's hands, though delayed a month, was that he'd broken his arm. But that she shouldn't tell their parents, or worry herself. Closing with the jaunty assurance that he would be home soon, and the first order of the day would be to have the bothersome bone properly set.

When I get home. How many times had she heard that? How many broken bones, knife wounds, burns of various degrees, and bullet holes had Ethan brought home with him? How many times had he scoffed at her concern with a hug and a kiss? And always with his grinning, dismissive drawl, "Don't worry your pretty little head about me, darlin'. I'm invincible, because I love you."

This had been the attitude and the unspoken reminder underlying the message Yancey had personally delivered just nights ago. Hearing them out loud, even if only in her own voice, not Ethan's, made angry tears well in her eyes. Dashing the stinging drops away, determined she wouldn't cry for her insufferable, beloved brother, she crossed her arms over her breasts and struggled to keep her promise.

"I won't cry, Ethan. I *won't!* Not for you or for..."

And there it was. The crux of her second problem, the second man who kept her awake nights.

Jackson Cade.

She'd tried to not think about him. Then, when he intruded into her thoughts against her will, she was determined to remember only his anger, only the disparaging insults. But it wasn't easy keeping at bay another vivid image of her unexpected nemesis. Of Jackson as he'd been at seventeen. Strong, broad, not as tall as his brothers but as handsome, with his dark auburn hair and brilliant blue eyes hiding amazing and unexpected flashes of green in their depths.

He'd danced with her, the scrawniest, newest, misfit kid, when no other boy at the school dance would. With his close-cropped hair gleaming like dark fire and his eyes more green than blue, he'd crossed the dance floor like a gallant knight, his armor a black tuxedo, his favor the rose from his boutonniere. The wallflower line held its collective breath, wondering who would be the chosen one this time.

When he stopped before her, Haley was sure it was some mistake, a cruel joke. Then he made a bow that should have seemed silly but was wonderful instead, offered her the rose— a rose she kept, still treasured—and led her into the crowd.

Without treading once on her toes, and never complaining when she planted a heel on his instep, he'd led her through the gliding steps of a slow waltz. Then a fast dance, and on and on through the night. Always making her look and feel as if she were the most graceful girl in the room. But he'd done more than dance with her, he'd talked as naturally as if they danced at every dance. And he'd drawn her out, and when she spoke, he listened.

When the evening was almost finished, as she ducked her head in answer to his good night, he didn't hurry away. Instead, with a finger at her chin, he'd raised her gaze to his.

You gotta show 'em. If you don't believe in yourself, whether it's that you're smart, or strong, or pretty, no one else will. As she'd recalled Ethan's message, Haley remembered the young Jackson's words now. Words she lived by. "You gotta show 'em."

The spoken repetition made her smile. Jackson Cade, young philosopher. Made wise beyond his years, perhaps by some hurt of his own. And perhaps in easing that hurt with kindness, along the way becoming a wallflower's dream.

He hadn't called her name. Everyone knew Jackson, and she'd been too nervous to think of her own. She realized now it was doubtful he ever knew it. She was simply another of Jackson's wallflowers. His kind deed for the night done, prophetic words uttered, he'd walked away and never looked back. And, obviously, he'd forgotten her completely.

But she'd never forgotten him. Dancing with him, really believing his words, became the turning point in her life. She wasn't in Belle Terre very long. That evening, her first and last school dance, was near the end. But she would carry the memory of both the city and the boy forever in her heart.

What she'd done with her life, what she'd accomplished, the strength to face an ordeal, refusing to let it destroy her, had come from within her. From trust in herself.

Strength and trust grounded in the gift of the rare wisdom of seventeen-year-old Jackson Cade. For that gift, and for the intuitive glimpse that showed her others hurt as she hurt and survived, she could forgive his moods, even his inexplicable anger, and hope that in time he would mellow.

"Mellow?" The very thought made Haley chuckle. Then chuckles gave way to laughter. "What on earth am I thinking? Jackson Cade mellow? Never!"

Long ago she'd decided he was likely born a firebrand. She understood now, with startling clarity, that beyond any doubt, he survived as a firebrand and he would die a firebrand.

And if she was falling in love with him again—as she had when he was seventeen and she fifteen—then she would simply have to learn to cope with the heat, to fight fire with fire.

She'd been too utterly amazed to admit, even to herself, what she'd seen and what she sensed. She admitted now, that beneath his anger and his mockery, there had been something in his eyes when he looked at her. Something that touched her as nothing ever had before, making her heart lurch, her breath falter.

A look that made her certain that the woman who tamed the firebrand would be loved as few women ever were. A wonderful, indefinable something that said she could be that woman.

"Is that it?" she mused as she looked down at the courtyard and the garden Linsey Stuart Cade called a lovers' bower. "Is Yancey right? Is that your problem with me, Jackson Cade? Am I a threat to some part of your well-ordered existence?"

A frown gathered between Haley's brows as she searched for answers she didn't have. "A threat...to what?" she mused. "And why? Is the answer in the look in your eyes?"

The last brought her to attention, mind and body keening

for answers. There was but one way to have them. One person held the key. "Just one," she muttered. "He lives at River Trace."

Spinning on her heel, leaving the open door and its panoramic view of Belle Terre and the lovers' garden, Haley stepped before a full-length mirror. Even on her day off, out of habit, she'd dressed for work. Boots, jeans, sensible shirt, a leather belt and vest. Her braid, her automatic solution for keeping what could be a wild mane under control and out of the way, hadn't yet begun to spring from the weave and thus was still neat.

Perfect for a barn call, she decided, as a determined look suddenly gleamed in her eyes and her cheeks flushed in anticipation of battle. "This is ridiculous, Haley Garrett," she warned the woman in the mirror one last time. "You're taking your life in your own hands. Perhaps his life, too."

Smoothing the vest over the slight ridge of her belt, she let her gaze fall on her unadorned and not-so-feminine fingers. Small, slender, but strong and capable as they had to be. "So?" She laughed softly. "What better strong and capable hands could either be in? Especially when a man doesn't have the good sense to know the right woman for him is only a smile and a kiss away."

Leaning closer to the mirror, she studied the blue-eyed woman. A woman who had been hurt and come out of the ordeal all the stronger. Learning along the way that doubt and fear and indecision accomplished nothing.

And if I should be hurt again? she wondered.

"You'll cope, Haley. And you'll survive," she told those questioning, doubtful blue eyes. "Then, as before, you'll go forward with your life. And no matter the hurt, you'll never look back mourning missed chances and lost love."

Crossing to her closet, she took out a small duffel, then tucked Merrie's clothes inside. She was ready to go.

With one last look in the mirror she paused, considering. Then, slipping two buttons of her shirt from their loops, she smiled and murmured, "Nothing ventured, nothing gained, but only a fool goes into battle unprepared.

"Full battle dress and fire with fire, Jackson," she promised, squaring her shoulders, tugging the gaping blouse and the vest taut across her breasts. "Oh, my, yes, my auburn-haired love, fire with fire. Faint heart never won this fair gentleman."

She was laughing, and but for Ethan, the ache of her sleepless nights had eased as she left the room.

After days of dreams and vacillation, now that her indecision had ended, the drive to River Trace seemed to take forever. The oaks she'd come to think of as sentries and the cathedral they formed were a pleasing, majestic sight. She knew from Lincoln and from Yancey that Belle Reve was an old Southern plantation that had always belonged to the Cade family. But River Trace was equally as old, surviving when the family had not.

The plantation had diminished until it was little more than a farm. Even that had fallen onto hard times when Jackson acquired it. The manor was still a work in progress. But one day River Trace would be complete again.

Until then, it was beautiful as it was, on this autumn day of decision. Leaving her car by the barn, Haley paused long enough to wonder where Jackson might be. Then, certain their paths would cross and war would likely be declared all over again, she walked the cobblestone path and stepped through the open door.

"Well, howdy and good morning, Doc."

Shading her eyes with a hand at her forehead and turning toward the familiar voice, Haley grinned at Jesse. "Good morning, Jesse. At least for now."

"Expecting fireworks, are you?"

"Does a wildcat have a stub for a tail?"

Setting aside a feed bucket, Jesse grinned and approached her. "What brings you here on this pretty day?"

"Just returning some clothes I borrowed." Her too innocent

tone made Jesse chuckle a little more heartily. "I've kept them so long, Merrie must be thinking I've absconded with them."

Jesse thumbed back his hat a notch and studied Haley's expression through narrowed eyes. "I reckon you're smart enough to know that Merrie's clothes are the least of your worries."

"Worry?" Linking her arm through his, she batted her eyes in an innocence meant to fool no one. "Who me?"

Jesse nodded and, with his gnarled cowboy's paw, patted her hand as it rested on his sleeve. "I take it, then, you've come loaded for bear. Or hothead."

"Something like that." Letting her amusement sound in her voice and warding off niggling and increasing apprehension, she glanced around. Except for Jesse and a few horses, the long barn seemed empty. "In the meantime, I'd like to see my patient."

"'Course you would. You won't believe how good Dancer looks, considering that mix of stuff he was given." Jesse had fumed for days over the toxicology report. The mix of substances should have killed Jackson's prize stud. He told anyone who listened that if Haley hadn't sedated the stallion, gambling that in a calmer state, his heart would outlast the effects of the drugs, Jackson would have lost more than a horse.

"He's feisty as a new colt in the cooler weather," Jesse elaborated. "With no small thanks to you, little girl."

"A lucky guess." Haley dismissed the feat as she always did.

"Humph. Maybe it was." Jesse walked with her toward Dancer's distant stall. "But in my book, that's what treating dumb animals is all about. A whole lot of guesswork, some good sense, and even more intuition. As far as guessing goes, anybody can guess," Jesse expounded, warming to his current favorite subject. "But I'll be first in line to tell you, little girl, not many have the gift of intuition. The day you moved to Belle Terre to practice with Lincoln was Jackson's lucky day."

"Tell him that." Haley's mouth curved in a wry smile.

"Wouldn't dare," the cowhand admitted as he stopped by the proper stall. "There's some things a feller like Jackson has to find out for himself."

"Just what is it I have to find out for myself, Jesse?" Jackson stepped from the corner of the stall, a curry comb in his hand. He didn't acknowledge Haley at all.

With a guileless expression at odds with the gleam in his eyes, Jesse shoved both hands into the back pockets of his jeans. "Why, that the doc is here, of course."

"So I see." Jackson's words were blunt, impatient. Then, with its flashes of green, the blue gaze Haley had found riveting and fascinating so many years ago settled on her. For a long moment he didn't speak or move and there was only the sound of horses, wonderful, handsome horses, shifting and shuffling and stamping. Even Jesse was silent and waiting.

On a deep breath, with a tilt of his head that might have been greeting, or not, Jackson asked, "What are you doing here?"

No hello, no how are you, no pleasantries. And whatever she'd thought she'd glimpsed in his eyes before was either well hidden beneath the sweep of his lashes or had never existed at all. Beyond in her imagination and in her wishful thinking, of course.

Stifling a sigh, realizing it was what she should have expected, Haley forced a nonchalant smile. "Since Lincoln's back in town, he insisted I take the day off. It's a beautiful day for a drive, so it seemed a logical time to return the clothing you borrowed for me from Merrie, as well."

"You drove all the way out here to return a scruffy pair of jeans and a shirt that could just as easily be returned in town?" Jackson's mocking look moved over her, taking in the snug fit of the vest and jeans, tarrying at the open shirt and the glimpse of the cleft that lay between tawny breasts.

Resisting the urge to reach for the edge of her vest, to pull it close over her shirt, with what aplomb she could muster, Haley explained, "I didn't have Merrie's address, and her number isn't listed in the book. As I said, it's a pretty day and…''

"And I'd asked her to stop by sometime to check a couple of horses for me," Jesse put in.

Jackson didn't look away from Haley as he addressed Jesse. "You called her, did you? Funny, I didn't realize we had problems with the horses. At least not anything you can't handle."

"Wasn't nothing major." Jesse was too old and too wily, and he knew Jackson too well, to be intimidated. "Just a few things I wanted the doc's opinion on. When she had time."

"So, on a pretty day for a drive, you just showed up?" Keeping Haley in his gaze, Jackson laid the comb aside, and absently stroked Dancer's nose as the stallion nudged his arm.

"Yes," Haley admitted calmly. Following Jesse's lead, she refused to let the angry tone of the question disturb her. "It would seem showing up unannounced is a failing we share."

"Touché." A slight grin ghosted over Jackson's face, then was gone so quickly one could almost imagine it had never happened. "As I recall, when I intruded, you were making dinner for Yancey." A brow slightly darker than his hair lifted in a sardonic attitude, as if her private little rendezvous was of no real interest to him, even as he asked, "A good evening?"

"I always enjoy my time with Yancey. He's one of the most interesting men I know." Haley watched as the second brow arched to match the other, this time in surprise. Since two could play this game, she turned the knife, just a little. "His adventures are so exciting. Sometimes one has to wonder if he's been everywhere and done everything."

"Yeah," Jackson agreed in a low snarl. "Twice."

Jesse made a strangled sound and tugged his hat down over his face, but not before Haley saw his teeth flash in a wide grin. Stepping closer to the stall, barely an arm's length away from Jackson, she turned her head, letting her braid fall over her shoulder to catch in the collar of her blouse. As his eyes tracked the path of the silver-and-gold rope of her hair with the curling ends lying against the naked swell of her breasts, she murmured softly, "I beg your pardon?"

As if her words scalded him, Jackson jerked back and looked away. Scowling, he snapped, "What?" Then scowling more fiercely, he added, "Why beg my pardon?"

"Jackson." Haley gestured with one hand, making it clear she didn't fathom his attitude. "I didn't understand what you said. I was merely..."

"How long have you known Yancey?" he interrupted.

"For some time."

"How long is that? A week, a month? Two? He isn't in town all that often. So one has to wonder if you really know him as well as you think you do. Even if you did seem rather chummy."

"'Chummy?'" Haley dared not look at Jesse, for she knew the old gossip was loving every minute and every word. Grinning in secret like an idiot, no doubt. Resting a hand on the door of the stall, aware of the not unpleasant mix of hay, horses, and the aftershave balm she seen in Jackson's bathroom, she curbed her own smile. "I'm not sure what you mean. Yancey's a friend. He has been for a number of years. He was in college with Ethan."

"Ethan?" In his agitation, forgetting that he'd heard the name before and wondering how many more men there were in her life, Jackson grumbled, "Ethan? Ethan who? Does he hug you and kiss you each time he's in range, too?"

"Ethan's my brother. Yes, he hugs me and kisses me, as Yancey does." Pausing for effect, she added, "Just not as often."

Jackson had stopped his absent petting of the stallion. Impatiently the massive creature stamped and snuffled and tossed his head, sending Jackson careening into the stall door. In an instinctive effort to keep his balance, he flung out a hand. Finding purchase, his fingers closed tightly, trapping Haley's hand between his and the top of the door.

"Ho, boy, ho. Settle down," he commanded the horse as he half turned to face it. After a second, when Dancer obeyed,

Jackson's attention fixed on Haley once more. His hand keeping hers, their gazes met, and all the anger seemed to drain from him. In a low voice, he said, "Sorry about that. Did I hurt you?"

Haley got the strong impression he was apologizing for more than this small incident. "No, Jackson, you didn't hurt me."

"As you see, Dancer's feeling more than a little frisky. Because of you." A nod included the cowhand, who had become strictly an observer. "And Jesse."

"It was the little girl's doing that saved the beast, Jackson. Not mine. Not yours." Jesse made the point, again, from his post a little distance away. "You know that."

"Yes." His fingers moved over the back of her hand, stroking the smooth flesh. Her braid lay now like a heavy cord against her breast. Her soft shirt clung to the lines of her body beneath the sleek black vest. Despite the sturdy faded jeans and the tall boots, she looked more like a model playing at being the sophisticated working woman than the real thing.

But as he turned her hand in his, cradling it as he stroked her palm, he found again the calluses that proved she was real, not an illusion. "Have I said thank you?"

Haley nodded, feeling the stroke across her palm down to her toes, and in all the sensuous places between. "At my house," she managed to say at last. "With gardenias."

"Then we're even?" His hand folded over hers, pulling both close to his body. "Neither of us owes the other anything?"

Haley nodded in agreement, wondering where this was going. "We're even."

Jackson took another deep breath, released her, then opened the stall and stepped out. "Good," he said in a low mutter. "Then we can go back to the letter of our truce. In keeping with that, now that you've delivered Merrie's clothes and answered Jesse's call for advice, you can try a little harder to keep your part of our bargain."

At her startled look, he explained in the long-suffering tone meant for the obtuse, "Your promise that you'd see to it our paths didn't cross any more than absolutely necessary. Does that sound familiar, Duchess?"

A stern look cast at Jesse dared him to make fodder for his gossip mill of this. Then, with a bleak smile and a half bow for Haley, he stalked from the barn into the noonday sun.

He was beyond hearing before Jesse scuffed a boot against the floor, shoved his hands into his pockets, and shook his head. With the habitual lift of his shoulders, he looked at Haley and grinned. "The man's bonkers and head over heels crazy over you. A drowning man, going down for the second time."

Haley laughed in euphoric delight. "I know."

"Other than his stubborn ways, how did you figger it out?"

"I didn't, at least not alone. Yancey told me."

"Yancey oughta know. He knows Jackson well enough."

"I hope so, Jesse. I really hope so."

"He's going to fight it, you know. The boy's got a burr under his saddle no one but him understands. But when he finally goes down, he'll go down hard." Taking off his hat, running his fingers around the band, he looked up at Haley. "I suspect he's just about there already."

"You think so?" Doubt colored her tone.

"Yep. Third time down is due real soon. But because he's suspecting it himself, he's as stubborn as he's going to get. So—" Jesse rubbed the stubble on his chin, a co-conspirator to the end "—how do you want to play it?"

"Cool. Aloof. Like he's the last man I would ever want in Belle Terre."

"But he ain't the last?" Jesse asked the question for one final assurance.

"No." Haley looked past the door, the cobblestone walk was empty. It had been empty for some time. Jackson was out of sight, but never out of her thoughts. "Not by a long shot."

"Mind some help? Right subtle-like help, that is? Nothing that would tip our hand."

"I'll take all the help I can get, Jesse."

"Long as you're sure the fire-eater is who you want."

The fire-eater. It didn't surprise her that Jesse viewed Jackson as she did. "I'm sure." Had she ever really had a choice? The disaster with Todd wasn't her fault, but perhaps settling for second choice had been her part of a mistake. "I think I've been sure since I was fifteen."

"That long, huh?" Jesse looked at her quizzically, but for once the consummate gossip didn't interrogate her.

"Yeah." Haley nodded. "That long."

"Then I'll see to it. Maybe talk to some of the fellers. Even his brothers. Don't think they would appreciate being left out of the fun."

"You think taming Jackson Cade will be fun?"

Jesse cocked a laughing eye at her. "Don't you?"

"If, in the end, he wants to be tamed."

"Oh, he will, little girl. Mark my word on it. He will." Jesse's grin faded. "Are you in a hurry? I got a thermos of cold water and a passel of sandwiches in my saddlebag. Compliments of Miz Corey over at Belle Reve. Want to ride with me, take a look at the herds we got scattered in the different pastures? There's a shade tree or two along the way that's just right for a picnic."

"I'm in no hurry to leave, but Jackson would prefer it."

"All the more reason for you to stay awhile. Besides, there's some pretty good-looking fellows tending them horses. If you go off and spend the day among them, he's bound to notice. Likely heat his blood up a little along with his temper.

"Expectin' such a time as this and figgerin' you for a rider, I cut a filly from the herd a couple of days ago. Got her in a back stall. Name's Sugar and she's in dire need of exercise."

"In that case, for myself and for Sugar, I'd be delighted. Should I take the clothes up to Merrie's room now, or later?"

Jesse reached for a bridle. "Later's better. After he knows where you've been." When she looked at him strangely, amusement became a laugh. "Hey. You don't think I'm the only gossip at River Trace, do you?"

"But just in case, you're going to make sure the right people know where we've gone.'' Haley decided Jesse was an ally made in heaven. ''The other gossips, right?''

''Girl.'' The bridle jangled as Jesse walked to the stall of a pretty mare. ''Nobody told me you were a mind reader, too.''

Six

By the cant of the sun, Haley knew her ride with Jesse had stretched longer than she'd intended. But weeks had passed since she'd been on a horse, and the hours had slipped away.

Jesse had taken her at her word, that it was a beautiful day for a ride. Not seeming to be in any hurry himself, he'd given her the grand tour of the pastures and land of River Trace, and some that lay beyond its boundaries. Along the way, he'd stopped to talk to the men in charge of the horses, and to those who still stood guard. Jericho's men, unobtrusive and ever wary.

In a shaded clearing, by a stream, they'd shared his lunch. And Haley wondered if peanut butter and strawberry jam, which she discovered were Jesse's favorite, had ever been so good. Later, tracking through the stream and across, he'd shown her the marker that was the cornerstone of four separate properties. River Trace, Belle Reve, land that had for years upon years been known simply as the Stuart farm. Each meeting acreage that once belonged to Eden's family, recently re-couped by Adams.

"Standing right here," Jesse had said, "for as far as you can see, the land belongs to one or the other of the Cades. None of it the youngest son's, of course. But I don't guess that matters, for someday Jefferson will go back to Arizona."

The day was like that, with small bits of knowledge shared, some true and, this being Jesse, some gossip. Lincoln had told her a little of his family when they were classmates and friends in the California Veterinary College. Then more when she'd turned her back on the failure of her life in Virginia and come to Belle Terre to start anew.

But it was Jesse who was most informative, as with a full belly, the warm sun at his back, and a good horse beneath him, he reminisced. As they rode at an easy pace, she learned he'd come to the lowcountry at Jefferson's request, meaning only to work awhile. But he stayed because the Cades had become his family, or as close as he would ever come to hav-ing one.

"It's peculiar how they're different but so much alike. Just on a glance, a stranger wouldn't put the Cades together as brothers. But spend a little time with them, watch, and listen, and only a dolt wouldn't know," Jesse had expounded, and Haley had listened with rapt interest. "The difference, I sup-pose, is from having different mothers. Maybe the sameness is in that none of the women was ever around. Adams's ma died of overwork. Lincoln's, from a fall. Jackson's and Jef-ferson's both just took off.

"Didn't seem to bother Jefferson too much. But Jackson?" Jesse shook his head as he reined his mount to a halt by the barn. "Something about it eats at the hellion."

"You don't know what or why?" Haley slid from the sad-dle. Gathering up the reins, she watched Jesse do the same. "He doesn't talk about it?"

"No." With Haley beside him, the cowhand walked to the barn. "And if you want to keep your head, don't ask."

"Do you…" Haley began, but stopped. "Never mind."

Jesse tossed her a quizzical look but said nothing until he reached for the reins. "Why don't you go on up to the house and put Merrie's clothes away? I'll see to your horse. It's getting late—I thought maybe you have a date. Daniel, maybe. Or Yancey. As I remember, Dr. Cooper likes you pretty good, too."

"My evening is free, Jesse. I've nothing better to do than see to Sugar here." Haley had already begun unbuckling the saddle. She stripped it off as she spoke.

"Shh, girl!" Jesse took the saddle over her protest. "Don't say that. At least not where some folks can hear. Of course you have a date. A heavy date."

Catching his intent, Haley paused for a thought, then nodded. "I do have a date of sorts. Cade called to tell me that Brownie and his wife have a new litter of puppies. I promised I would stop by to see them one day soon."

"No better day than today," Jesse suggested. "So you'd best run along to the house. No one's likely there this time of day, so just step on in. Merrie's room is the little one off the kitchen, you can't miss it. So scat. Remember to give my regards to young Cade and Mister and Miz Brownie and the pups."

"Jesse." Haley stood on tiptoe to kiss his weathered cheek. "You're a genius, and a handsome scoundrel in the bargain."

"Of course." Jesse touched his cheek as she dashed away.

The house was quiet, and her knock had gone unanswered. As Jesse suggested, Haley opened the kitchen door and stepped inside. The room was functional, but the appliances were old and yellowed. Jackson's planned renovations obviously hadn't reached this part of the house. But, then, what need did a determinedly confirmed bachelor have for a fancy kitchen?

Setting down the duffel, she took one place setting of dishes from the table, washed and rinsed them, and set them in the drainboard to dry. Beyond that, little else was out of place. Jackson was neat but not obsessive. And, she realized, a little too late, he certainly didn't need her meddling in his routine. A woman's touch was the last thing he seemed to want in his life.

Catching up the bag, she paused, orienting herself. The arch would lead to the rest of the house. A very narrow door likely opened into a pantry. The one remaining interior door, as she supposed, led to Merrie's room.

Like the kitchen, the room was old and quaintly plain, but for the personal touches Hayley knew must have been added by the young student. There was no closet, and she didn't want to rummage through dresser drawers. Instead, she laid the borrowed garments on the pillow of the narrow bed that was little more than a cot.

As she straightened from the task, a picture in a heavy frame caught her eye. Of a horse, of course. Haley smiled at that. But the striking creature was flanked on one side by one of the most exquisite young women she'd ever seen, and a handsome man on the other.

Taking it from the bedside table, as she brought it closer, she knew it could only be Merrie Alexandre with Jackson, both in the formal dress of a horse show. A heavy trophy stood at their feet. He was smiling, as he'd never smiled at her.

The threat of inexplicable tears closed around her throat at the same time as powerful hands gripped her shoulders.

Stifling a scream, as old habits and old memories came flooding back, in equally habitual silence she turned to fight. The heavy frame bounced against the table, then the floor. Shattering glass and harsh breathing were the only sounds within the small, confined space.

"No!" a low, deep voice rumbled in stumbling apology. "Everything's okay. You're okay. Don't be afraid."

Haley was too intent on escape to hear or comprehend.

"Listen, Duchess. *Listen.*" The hands that had grasped her shoulders caught her wrists, firmly but gently pulling her hands from his face. "I'm sorry. I didn't know...I didn't mean..." Because she still didn't hear him, still didn't comprehend, and her panic didn't subside, Jackson folded her in his arms. Trapping her against his body, he held her, closely. Patiently, gently, he held her, until, like a small, captured bird, exhausted by panic itself, her struggles grew weaker, then weaker.

Stroking her hair, he whispered to her. A singsong rhythm of broken thoughts and broken phrases. "You're safe. It's me…only me…just Jackson."

Hearing his own name, remembering how he'd treated her, he wondered what credible reassurance he could give her. "I didn't mean to frighten you."

A lie, or almost. He had meant to startle her and catch her off guard. But he hadn't expected anything like this reaction. Never anything like this. Haley was not the nervous, skittish sort of woman. This, he knew deep in his gut, was far more. Far worse. An instinctive reaction. A learned response.

Learned at her expense. And Jackson had no doubt he knew the price she'd paid. Five ugly scars that were never very far from his thoughts of late loomed in his mind. An obscene flower, a barbaric brand of unspeakable cruelty.

"God forgive me," he muttered in a guttural tone. "I'm sorry." As she went suddenly still, drawing her head down to his chest, he brushed her hair with his lips. He couldn't hold her close enough, or say the words enough to ease the ache those scars branded across his own heart. "My poor, brave Duchess, I'm sorry."

She didn't speak, or acknowledge that she knew him, or that she understood his regret. Yet her arms crept slowly around his waist. Her hands sliding beneath the untucked tail of his open shirt clutched at his back, fingernails curling and sinking like short daggers into flesh still damp from his abandoned shower. In a death grip, she clung to him in need born of terror.

In the aftermath, she was trembling.

More than anything, that strong, foolishly courageous Haley Garrett trembled was his undoing. The genesis of her reaction was buried deeply, and had nothing to do with him. But he was the catalyst. For that he damned himself. For that, what comfort he could offer he would give—if it meant holding her through the twilight and the coming night, then he would hold her.

Careful of the glass, he guided her a single step to the cot. Sinking down on its edge, he gathered her closer, held her tighter, murmuring, again, the broken words of remorse.

He lost all concept of time. For Jackson, there was only Haley, her trembling body pressed against his, her hands touching him, clinging to him. Too aware of the softness of her breasts lying against his naked chest, he struggled to control his own rapidly igniting needs.

Instead, in an exercise in futility, he concentrated on the room. Built more than a century ago, intended as temporary lodgings for temporary kitchen help, the room was small, close, with space for only a narrow bed and the dresser. At morning and noon, it could be gloomy. In the evening the sun filled it with broken light and moving shadows of dancing leaves, creating the rare magic of chiaroscuro. Which reminded him of the woman he held. Bringing him full circle, as in defeat, he could not help but admire the shimmer of shade and light playing over her hair, setting the heavy braid and the escaping strands aglow.

Silvered gold. He hadn't believed such a thing was possible, until Haley. He hadn't believed he could ever feel as he did, here, now, with a woman the likes of which he'd never known. With any woman. Yet, as her trembling eased and gradually ceased, as the punishing grip of her hands relaxed, as she curled into him like a lost kitten seeking a gentle hand, every promise he'd made to himself too many years before shattered into dust.

He didn't want to remember the past, or old promises. Not here. Not now. What he wanted was to loosen her hair from the band holding her braid. He wanted to comb it free of the restraining weave with his fingers and feel the strands slip like silk over his palms. He wanted to slay the demon he'd awakened and lay it to rest forever. He wanted to hold her as he held her now, forever. He wanted to kiss her and beg forgiveness.

In this small, aged room, he wanted to make love to her, forgetting the old, old hatreds and prejudices that had colored his young life and set the standard of the man he had become. He struggled against the overwhelming desire to bury himself in her, to become a part of her, letting the softness and the gentle strength so alien to him slay his own demons.

He wanted so much he couldn't have. The very thing he'd made impossible—Haley's unguarded friendship, and her love.

So, against his own will, he dreamed impossible dreams.

Impossible or not, he wasn't ready to let her go. But too soon, she caught a startled breath and pushed away, her hands moving from his back to rest against his bare chest. More than anything, he wanted to bring her back.

"Jackson," she murmured, as if she were surprised to see him. Her eyes were half hidden beneath heavy lids and the sweep of gold tipped lashes. Slowly, as if she'd forgotten, she realized where she was and what had happened. "Oh, dear heaven." A flush colored her pale cheeks. "You must think I'm a brazen fool."

"'Brazen.'" He repeated her word. In it there was no hint of what he was feeling.

With a slight pressure, she tried to lever herself away from any contact with him. But, refusing to let her go, he caught her hands in his, keeping them against his bare chest. Expecting angry agreement to her self-disparagement, she looked away. At anything, but him. Her gaze fell on the picture of Jackson smiling as he never smiled at her.

"Why would I think you were brazen, Haley?"

"Why?" Tearing her attention from the replica of his smile, she considered his question. If her hands had been free, she would have gestured toward the room and beyond. "For coming into your home, and into Merrie's room uninvited and unwelcome. For ruining a special remembrance."

When he said nothing, compelled to fill the electric silence between them, she tried to explain. "I knocked. When there was no answer, assuming, as Jesse had suggested, no one was home at this hour, I thought it wouldn't hurt to slip inside and…"

"Leave Merrie's clothes," he finished for her. "I didn't hear you knock, Haley. I was just stepping from a shower when I heard another sound. The creak of a board, something." His fingers moved over hers as he breathed in the scent of fresh air and Haley. "Merrie is deep into a special project and isn't coming this week. So, knowing it wouldn't be her, and given recent events, I came to investigate."

"And found me. The last person you want in your house. An intruder of the worst sort." The gaze she lifted to his was bleak, holding shadows of remorse and the aftermath of fear. "I'm sorry I intruded. Sorry I reacted as I did. Sorry I thought…"

With a dismissive shake of her head, her fingers convulsed into fists beneath his. Her nails scraped against his chest, lightly, inadvertently, sending barely controlled shards of need and desire spiraling through him again. Jackson knew he should let her go. But he couldn't. Not yet. Not until he knew.

"What did you think, Duchess?"

The terror of the moment of his first touch was still too raw. The weakness she thought she'd gotten past too disturbing. Looking anywhere but into a gaze that would see too much, she lifted a suddenly weary shoulder, trying to dismiss what couldn't be so easily dismissed. "I was reacting, not thinking."

Reacting out of fear. No, far worse than fear, Jackson was certain. He'd felt it in her trembling body. He saw it now in the lingering vestiges of horror still clouding her eyes.

Fear of what? Of whom? Of the past he'd begun to suspect. Of memories of the despicable monster who left his mark on her? Or of him? Dear God, he wondered, was Haley that afraid of him?

The thought clawed at him, twisting in him like the sword of retribution, leaving him as shaken as she. That he might have caused this...that she would even think he could hurt her.... Shame such as he'd never known seized his heart and his mind. The ache of tears he hadn't shed since he was fourteen burned his eyes and were banished only by the lowering guard of his lashes.

He was afraid to ask, afraid to hear her answer. But he had to know. Sliding his fingers through the loose tendril that escaped her braid, cradling her head with gentle fingers, he lifted her face to his. He needed to see her mobile, expressive face, to see what was there as she answered the question that could damn him forever in his own eyes. "Are you afraid of me, Haley? Have I done this to you?"

He saw the sudden spark of surprise in her eyes, in her wonderful, hurting eyes. "What could you have done to me, Jackson? Why would you even think you could affect me at all?"

"This. That we're sitting here in a small, dark room. That you fought me." Ruefully, as he folded the fingers of one hand around her wrist, to insure that she didn't flee from him, he stroked his cheek. A row of angry scratches roughened the place near where his finger moved. Beading droplets of vermilion, too tiny to do more than ooze, were drying along the trails left by her nails. Blood that wouldn't fall or drip, but would tomorrow and for many days to come be a reminder of this single day.

With a stricken expression she followed the path of his long, sun-darkened, work-roughened finger. With eyes filled with regret for the harm she'd inflicted to his handsome features, in a voice little more than a sighing breath, she whispered, "I didn't know." A shake of her head left the rest unsaid. "I'm sorry."

A word they'd both said too much and too often in one day. A word she shouldn't feel the need to say, Jackson decided. "What didn't you know, Haley? Was it, perhaps, who it was who touched you?" Not waiting for an answer. "Or worse, did you not know what that person, whoever it was, might do to you?"

"No," she protested, even as her eyes made her protest a lie. A desperate lie.

Ignoring her denial, he asked with renewed gentleness that, even so, could not soften the battering questions, "In that startled instant, did you forget where you were? Did you forget that even though an arrogant, opinionated imbecile and literally a son of a bitch might live at River Trace, no monsters did? Certainly not the monster from your past."

"Monsters?" Haley jerked away from him then, and would have pulled free had he not anticipated that exact reaction. "Now you're imagining things."

"Am I, Duchess?" He spoke as softly as he had when he both soothed and corrected Dancer. His voice as calm, as mesmerizing, even as it probed. "Am I imagining the marks left by an innately gentle woman, and the desperation that overruled that gentleness, turning her into a warrior?"

"There are no monsters, here or in my past. I'm not a warrior." She wanted to laugh, mocking him as he'd mocked her, but her mouth and throat wouldn't obey. "I was startled."

He laughed, a sound without humor. "In case you haven't noticed, sweetheart, this went farther than just being startled."

"I overreacted. I've not been sleeping well." Even to Haley, the excuses seemed weak. For distracting effect, she added, "I was also in enemy territory, and on edge."

"'Enemy territory?'" A doubting, questioning brow lifted. "Yet you came?"

"Not one of my better decisions. Next time I'll send Merrie's clothes to Eden. Or find a way to return them myself."

"'Next time?'" Because he knew there would be no answers, this day, regarding the monster in her past, Jackson let himself be distracted, and chose to create a little distraction himself. A distraction he shouldn't allow but couldn't resist.

Stroking back her hair, watching a ray of the sun tangle in it, he leaned closer. "Then you know there will be next time."

"I misspoke." Haley wanted to move away, to put a safe space between them. But she couldn't. Nor could she look away from the face of the man she'd loved for more than half her life. "After today, I intend to keep my promise."

"To see that our paths never cross any more than they must?" He was closer, his clasp still circled her wrists. But not in a grip she couldn't break if she tried.

"Yes." Like a child repeating what she must learn by rote, she said, "Never more than they must."

"But when they do? What shall *we* do?"

"We'll be civil." He was so close, the clean scent of his body enveloped her and seemed to caress her senses as his fingers were suddenly caressing her wrist.

"Civil?" he asked, amused. "As in civilized?"

"Of course."

"Is this civilized?" In a way she couldn't fathom because she could barely think at all when his mouth nearly brushed hers, with one hand he opened her fingers and pressed them against his bare skin. His heart lay beneath her fingertips, the rhythm strong, sure, too fast. "Is it civilized when your touch does this to me? Can we be civilized any more than we can be friends, with this between us?"

"No." She protested, not his words but that he was pulling her to him. He'd released his grasp at last, but only to take her in his arms. God help her, he was going to kiss her, and she dared not let him. For then he would know. And in his teasing he would have made her the fool he'd always thought.

"No?" he murmured as if he understood, even as he asked, "Does that mean no we can't be civilized, or no…"

Her breath came in unsteady gasps as she reached for one last shred of control. "It means there's nothing between us."

"Isn't there?" Jackson laughed softly, seductively. "Little warrior, let me show you."

He pulled her closer. The tips of her breasts had brushed his bare chest…now there was not even breathing room between them. Her body seemed to cleave to his with a will of its own, no matter that her mind knew it was wrong, a mistake. In one last effort at sanity, tossing back her head, intending to rebuff him, she gave him the opportunity he was waiting for.

The last thing she saw as he bent to her was blue eyes alight with green fire.

Slowly, as if he had all the time in the world, his head dipped to hers. His breath warmed her cheek in a sweet prelude to his kiss. When his lips touched hers, there was no trace of the angry man he'd been. No hint of mockery. Nothing of the kiss she'd dreamed a kind young boy's would be. This was the kiss of a mature man. The brand of a man who wanted a woman.

Like or dislike, respect or scorn, Jackson wanted her. As he'd warned, there was nothing civilized in his need. As the knowledge sank in, shock held her motionless. When in a rush of fear she would have torn her mouth from his, a twist of his palm coiled her braid into his grasp. The tug of it keeping her.

When she took a breath with the foolish thought to object, he seized the opportunity and made the most of it. His tongue stroked hers, demanding and yet an intimate caress.

Haley forgot her protest, and the fear that had held her so tightly in its suffocating grip. She forgot her reason for coming to this tiny room of sunstruck gloom, and that she had trespassed. Most of all, she forgot that only hours ago she'd believed the man who kissed her as if he would possess all of her—body, mind, heart and soul—would be a reluctant lover.

Most of all, she forgot the game Jesse proposed. As if with minds and needs of their own, her hands glided over his ribs to the corded muscles of his arms and shoulders. Without consciously thinking, she wondered how such contained strength could be such a tender prison.

A prison she didn't want to escape as her hands continued their quest, stopping only when her palms cupped his nape. Her fingertips brushing the close-cropped auburn mane, even as the pressure of her touch brought his mouth harder against hers, making his kiss even deeper, more impassioned.

Her legs were trembling, her knees were weak. Were they not half sitting, half lying on Merrie's cot, she wondered if she would have fallen. A bed not meant for lovers, but a bed, nevertheless. The idea made her body ache with the sort of torment only Jackson could ease. A low groan sounded in her throat as her fingers tightened, keeping him. Wishing he would never leave her.

Jackson heard the low, sweet sound. He heard the need. His kiss grew gentle. His arms were no longer a prison but a haven as he touched her face and stroked her hair. Pulling away, but only enough to skim his fingers down the length of her braid to free it from the banded restraint.

Haley thought vaguely of protesting again, but his muttered, anticipating *No,* and a trail of kisses down her throat and across her shoulder swept the thought further from her mind.

Then the band was gone, fluttering like a butterfly to the floor, as impatient fingers combed and stroked flyaway strands in a hypnotic rhythm. "Sunlight," he whispered, remembering. "I've always thought your hair was captured sunlight."

Haley laughed huskily, the sound of it fading as the stroking fingers of one hand tangled in her hair, bringing her back to him. But not as close as he would have her. Letting his free hand glide down the length of her body to her hip, her thighs, then her knees, he lifted her to his lap.

She was light and shadow. In her caress were sweet promises. Promises he would take, and tomorrow be damned. With his face buried in the cascade of her hair, and his fingertips hovering at the curve of her breasts, he breathed in the scent of her and, with the last of a faltering gallantry, sought tacit consent. "Duchess, sweet Duchess, I need…"

The slap of the kitchen door resounded like a shot. A sound that shredded what Haley realized with sickening immediacy could only be a passing fantasy. Footsteps crossed the kitchen, sounding too loud in the still of early evening, as she pulled away from Jackson and stood looking down at him, but only briefly.

"Doc?" Jesse called from nearby as she stooped to scoop up the band for her hair but found Jackson was there before her. When she reached for it, his fingers folded it into his palm.

Then it was too late. Jesse stood in the doorway, watching curiously. "I thought by now you had left for your date," he said, at last. "Then I saw your truck."

What Haley drove was officially called a SUV. A sports

utility vehicle, and perfect for her work. But she didn't correct
Jesse, for even she referred to it as a truck. "There was no
answer when I knocked," she managed to rasp in a scratchy
voice. "So, as you suggested, I came on in. I was just putting
Merrie's clothes away."

"When I frightened her," Jackson added as he came to
stand beside her.

Jesse's hooded look traveled over them, not missing Haley's
loose hair, or that Jackson was half dressed and his face was
scratched. "You frightened her."

It wasn't a question, but Jackson answered. "I was taking
a shower and didn't hear her knock. Later, I heard a sound
and came to investigate. Haley wasn't expecting anyone."

The old cowhand nodded as if the explanation made perfect
sense, then said wryly, "It's been a spell since the doc came
to the house. Took you a while to investigate, did it?"

"I broke the glass in the picture." Haley was babbling and
she knew it. "I was going to clear it away."

"With Jackson's help, of course."

"We were deciding how to handle the matter when you
came in," Jackson said smoothly, without a prayer of fooling
Jesse.

"I see," Jesse said, and he did see. Far too much. "Then
why don't you take care of it now, and let the doc head on
out? She looks a mite under the weather for a heavy date."

"Of course," Jackson agreed as he, too, saw the pallor that
had washed away the flush his lovemaking had incited. Her
eyes had the dry shine of panic.

Now that sanity had returned, feeling a wanton fool, she
seized the chance to escape. "If you don't mind, I think I will
leave." Her gaze collided with Jackson's, but she couldn't
read what was in his eyes. "I shouldn't have intruded. The
whole day was a mistake. I shouldn't have come to River
Trace.

"I'm sorry for all I said." Realizing she'd said hardly anything, that she hadn't tried, or been given the chance, she
amended, "Sorry for the picture and...and for all I did."

Turning abruptly, she fled from the room. It was Jesse's call

Play the

"LAS VEGAS"

GAME

GET 3 FREE GIFTS!

FREE GIFTS!

FREE GIFTS!

FREE GIFTS!

TURN THE PAGE TO PLAY! Details inside! →

Play the

"LAS VEGAS" Game

and get

3 FREE GIFTS!

FREE GIFTS!

FREE GIFTS!

1. Pull back all 3 tabs on the card at right. Then check the claim chart to see what we have for you — 2 FREE BOOKS and a gift — ALL YOURS! ALL FREE!

2. Send back this card and you'll receive brand-new Silhouette Desire® novels. These books have a cover price of $3.99 each in the U.S. and $4.50 each in Canada, but they are yours to keep absolutely free.

3. There's no catch. You're under no obligation to buy anything. We charge nothing — ZERO — for your first shipment. And you don't have to make any minimum number of purchases — not even one!

4. The fact is, thousands of readers enjoy receiving their books by mail from the Silhouette Reader Service™. They enjoy the convenience of home delivery...they like getting the best new novels at discount prices, BEFORE they're available in stores...and they love their *Heart to Heart* newsletter featuring author news, horoscopes, recipes, book reviews and much more!

5. We hope that after receiving your free books you'll want to remain a subscriber. But the choice is yours — to continue or cancel, any time at all! So why not take us up on our invitation, with no risk of any kind. You'll be glad you did!

Visit us online at
www.eHarlequin.com

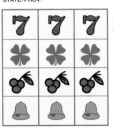

The Silhouette Reader Service™ —Here's how it works:

If offer card is missing write to: Silhouette Reader Service, 3010 Walden Ave., P.O. Box 1867, Buffalo, NY 14240-1867

BUSINESS REPLY MAIL
FIRST-CLASS MAIL   PERMIT NO. 717-003   BUFFALO, NY

POSTAGE WILL BE PAID BY ADDRESSEE

SILHOUETTE READER SERVICE
3010 WALDEN AVE
PO BOX 1867
BUFFALO NY 14240-9952

NO POSTAGE
NECESSARY
IF MAILED
IN THE
UNITED STATES

that brought her up short. "I'll call you, little girl. We have some discussing to do."

"No, Jesse. We have nothing more to discuss. I was mistaken, I can't do as we planned."

The last of her answer was still ringing in the air when the back door closed behind her. Jackson stared at the place where she'd stood, then turned a laser glare on Jesse. "What was that about? What mistake did the Duchess make? What plan?"

"Wasn't nothing." Jesse lifted a shoulder, a sure sign he would say only what he wanted to say and not one word more.

"Nothing, huh?" Jackson murmured as the engine of her truck sounded through the quiet. "A mighty disturbing nothing."

"She'll be all right," Jesse declared as he crossed to the door and stopped. "I'll get the broom and dustpan and help you clear that away."

When he was alone, Jackson listened to the fading sound of an engine and remembered an inexplicable panic. "Will she, Jesse?" he wondered out loud as he knelt to gather up broken glass. "As long as she's so frightened, can she ever be all right?"

"Talkin' to yourself, Jackson?"

"Yes." No engine disturbed the quiet. Not even a trace of the clean scent of her hair remained in the room. "I suppose I am."

"Too bad Doc had a date."

Through gritted teeth Jackson growled, "Would you shut up about her blasted date!"

Jesse said nothing, and they worked in silence, together. Until he cast a sly glance at Jackson, asking, "How you gonna explain that your face looks like you got crossways of a wildcat?"

"I'll say I got crossways of a wildcat, what else?"

Chuckling, Jesse drawled, "That oughta work. Specially since wildcats are scarcer than hen's teeth in the lowcountry."

Seven

"Drat!"

Jackson heard the too familiar word tumble from his lips and looked from the tie that defeated him to the startled gaze he saw in the mirror. Startled because for once he was thinking of a woman other than one who had haunted his thoughts by day and his dreams at night.

With a will of its own, the image of Haley Garrett had filled his mind for days...with a constancy that left little room for thoughts of anyone or anything else. Except now, with the formal tie. And like everyone of a certain station who'd been a child in Belle Terre, Jackson's thoughts turned to Lady Mary and her dictum on formal dress.

He'd been eight when he joined Adams and Lincoln in the twice-weekly classes of deportment the elderly lady conducted in the aged and faded townhouse that had belonged to her family for more than a century. Irascible Gus Cade insisted his sons learn the meticulous ways of Belle Terre society. And learn they did, if they knew what was good for their backsides.

"Even how to tie a dratted tie. When it will behave." Hearing the only word of irritation Lady Mary allowed herself, Jackson smiled. An act as rare in the last week as the hen's teeth Jesse liked to speak about.

Hen's teeth segued into wildcats and scratches. And with more frequency than he wanted to admit, Haley was there again, filling his mind. Leaning closer to the mirror, he inspected the nearly healed marks left by her nails. Marks that generated curiosity. Too much curiosity, especially among his brothers. And, of course, Yancey would drop by in one of his rare visits to River Trace when they were at their flaming best.

"Wildcat," he murmured what had been his steadfast and unrecanted answer to the fiendish teasing of both family and friends. Unrecanted and not a lie, for in the more than seven days since he'd seen her, he'd come to realize that the name fit her as well as Duchess. "A fighter as well as a lady."

He hadn't forgotten the deep wells of terror and panic her eyes had become when she'd turned to fight. But that she *had* turned to fight, not folded—that was the telling element.

"You screwed up, buster," he told his own grim image in the mirror. "The first woman to get past the barbed-wire fence erected around your heart, and you screwed up."

Suddenly too angry to deal with the stubborn tie, he jerked his hands away and left it to dangle over the precise tucks of his formal shirt. Lincoln had the right idea. Tonight another Cade would follow his tradition, seeking out Lady Mary, listening as she tied their ties and scolded. Even though she wasn't fooled for a minute. Lady Mary, better than any, knew how well she'd honed away the rough edges of Gus Cade's half-wild sons.

"Lady Mary it is," Jackson muttered as he turned away from the mirror and picked up his jacket.

"I swear, boy, if you keep talkin' to yourself, we're gonna have to find you a keeper," Jesse drawled from the open doorway where he lounged against the doorjamb.

A Jesse like none Jackson had ever seen. "Jesse! What are you doing here, dressed like that?"

"I'm here checking up on you, of course." Pushing away from the jamb, with a grunt of amusement the cowhand looked down at himself. "What's the matter with the way I'm dressed, Jackson? Is my slip showing?"

"Slip? Hardly." Jackson nearly choked on the words, for Jesse's exactly fitted, obviously dated, formal attire was perfect and far from feminine. He could have stepped out of one of the glossy magazine or television advertisements featuring ruggedly attractive, versatile Westerners. "You're going to Eden's gala for the children's wing of the hospital."

"Bingo!" Jesse grinned. "Give the man a cigar."

"Why?"

"Why not?" The perfect Westerner didn't explain the sly plan he would set into motion tonight with the help of Jackson's brothers and friends.

"You've never been before," Jackson pointed out.

"Never had a date with a beautiful lady for one of Eden's galas before, either."

"You have a date?"

"Don't act so surprised." Jesse gave a mock scowl. "I clean up pretty good, if I do say so myself. And, just for tonight, I won't eat my peas with one of Eden's silver knives."

"I doubt she'll have peas. This is a fund-raising event." Jackson was hardly aware of his comment as curiosity consumed him.

"I know that, boy." Jesse was maddeningly patient, as if Jackson were simple. "When I try, I can even speak low-country lingo with my pinkie raised over the handle of a punch cup."

"Who's the beautiful lady?" Jackson blurted.

"Well, now." Jesse slipped back into his Western drawl as easily as he slipped out. "'Pears to me that's my business. But the sooner we get that tie fixed, the sooner we can both go. Then you can see for yourself who the lady is."

"You can tie a bow tie?"

"Can't everybody?" Jesse asked, and proved that he could.

* * *

The Inn at River Walk, once the city home of Eden's family, was at its festive best. Eden's gifted skills melded with those of Cullen Pavaouau, the Pacific islander who was her best friend, her confidant, and her chief steward, so the house and gardens were, as always, quietly spectacular. On the mild and comfortable autumn evening, an eclectic crowd had already gathered.

At a glance, Jackson saw a farmer, a senator, a grocer, and an art collector. On a bench nearby, Jericho River's mother and Lady Mary listened as his grandmère, Letitia Rivers, the outrageous, outspoken grand dame of Belle Terre, held court.

Lincoln was present, with his tie immaculately tied. At his side was Linsey, his wife, the woman who had brought him a son and a wealth of love. Beyond them, Adams spoke with Jefferson and Merrie and kept a watchful eye on Eden at the same time.

There was no sign of Haley. The sound of new arrivals made Jackson realize that in his search he was blocking the main thoroughfare leading to the garden. Moving aside, he waited to speak to Jericho and his glowing, very expectant Maria.

"Jackson." Jericho's massive hand engulfed his. "How are you? How are things at River Trace?"

"Better," he answered, dropping a kiss on Maria's cheek and murmuring how utterly lovely she was in her pregnancy. "It will be better still when the guards can be called off."

"Which may not be long. We got a tip," Jericho explained. "If it pans out, the troubles at River Trace may be over."

"I won't hold my breath."

"A good idea." Jericho guided Maria away to speak to Eden.

As the crowd parted—which a crowd always did for a man with the presence and size of Jericho—Jackson saw her. "Haley."

He hadn't seen her because she was surrounded by four men, all nearly a foot taller. If he'd been in a better mood, the odd mix of the attentive group would have amused him. Daniel Corbett stood at her right. Davis Cooper and Yancey closed ranks in front of her. Jesse stood at her left.

"Musician and conductor, surgeon and lady's man, bad boy and bomb expert," Jackson recited the present version of 'Doctor, lawyer, Indian chief.' "Not to forget the cowboy."

Who, incredibly, seemed to be her date. "What the hell?"

"Talking to yourself, brother?" Lincoln stood at his elbow, a cup of punch in each hand.

"If one more person asks me that…"

"Does that mean it's become a habit?"

"Maybe." Never looking away from Haley, Jackson took the cup Lincoln offered, drank deeply, then began to cough and sputter. "Good Lord, Lincoln. This is Cullen's special brew!"

"You looked like you needed it." Wry amusement on his face, Lincoln sipped a much less robust punch than the islander's infamous and potent brew. "Especially once you saw who was Haley's escort. By the way, what happened to your face?"

"You asked that already, remember? I tangled with a wildcat." He handed the cup to Lincoln. "Hold this."

"Hey." Quietly, so no one but Jackson could hear, Lincoln called after him, "You're going the wrong way. Your usual ladies are over by the goldfish pond."

"No, *you're* wrong, my lady's standing with the unofficial bachelor society of Belle Terre." The second the possessive words were spoken, Jackson wondered where the impossible thought had come from. Then there was no more time to think. He was standing before her, among her other admirers.

"Jackson," she said as calmly and as controlled as if the mark of the disaster of their last meeting did not still score his cheek. "I didn't see you arrive."

"Of course not. You were a bit too busy." He nodded coolly to each of the men he normally considered good friends. He could forgive their competitive attention. Almost. For this was Haley Garrett as he'd seen her only once before.

Tonight, for this most special occasion, she wore a simple

gown, long, sleek, streamlined. A column of clinging, flame-colored fabric, and all the more attractive in its simplicity. A row of tiny pearl buttons, most of which were never meant to be closed, extended from a barely fitted band beneath her breasts to the middle of her throat. A smaller version of the same buttons, these held securely in their moorings, were repeated again from elbow to wrist on the long, slim sleeves.

Beyond a single stylus of ebony and pearl holding her hair in a loose coil at her crown, the buttons were her only adornment. He'd never seen her so lovely, or so fragile. At first he thought it was that he was accustomed to seeing her in bulkier jeans and vests rather than supple, clinging gowns that made her seem slimmer. Closer inspection of her face proved the thought a lie.

Haley's small and slender frame was, indeed, more slender. Which meant she was working too hard, driving herself. Perhaps to quiet her own personal demons.

If he could have his way, he would take her away from the gala and the joviality that threatened to exhaust her even more. If he could have his way, he would hold her and keep her close, insuring that she rested. But in that lay the greatest fallacy of all, for he knew that if he were alone with her, if he touched her, there would be no rest for either of them.

The encounter in Merrie's room proved that. A touch, a kiss, and he would make love to her. He couldn't stop himself, nor would Haley. That, too, had been proven at River Trace.

But he wouldn't take her away. He wouldn't be alone with her or hold her. For he didn't know what the attraction meant. Or, Jackson Cade being his mother's son, how long it would last. She'd been hurt enough sometime, somewhere, in ways he couldn't change, by someone he would like to strangle. He couldn't erase the past, but he could see to it he didn't hurt her again in the new future she'd carved out for herself in Belle Terre.

As conversation flowed around him, he'd smiled and nodded and hadn't heard a word. But he heard the music when it began. Certain he could risk holding her and touching her in the safety of a crowded dance floor, he stepped forward. With the slight, gallant bow that came so naturally to him, he murmured, "May I have the honor of this dance, Duchess?"

It hadn't occurred to him she would refuse, or even that she might not have a free dance. Not until he saw her stricken look and the flush that swept over her face. "I'm sorry, Jackson, I promised the first dance to Jesse."

"To Jesse," he said, as if the name didn't register.

"I can dance, you know," Jesse drawled, more pleased by Jackson's attitude than disturbed. "And I did bring the lady."

Wondering what happened to the tradition that the more graceful a cowboy was on a horse, the clumsier he would be afoot, Jackson watched as Jesse led her through the steps of the dance. "Jesse and Haley. Who would have believed it?"

"Yeah, who?" Davis Cooper agreed.

When Jackson followed the direction of Cooper's gaze, he knew which dancer interested the dauntless womanizer. "Don't even think it, Coop," he warned. "She isn't in your league."

"I'm going to dance with her, Jackson. Just dance." Cooper grinned. "In fact I have the next dance, and the sixth."

"The sixth?" Jackson asked in a low growl. "Which means?"

"It means," Yancey explained, "that we divvied up her dances. Jesse, as you see, has first. Coop, second. I'm third."

"I got the fourth," Daniel chimed in. "Then the rotation begins all over again."

"The hell it does." Jackson sent a withering look at his friends. "If you had a brain between you, you'd see the Duchess is too tired to be divvied up as if she were your private harem."

"Not so private," Coop suggested a little too innocently, but Jackson was too disturbed to notice. "Adams asked her to save him a dance, so did Jefferson and Lincoln. And—"

"We'll see about that." Not caring that he disturbed the dancers, Jackson stalked across the temporary dance floor constructed in a clearing beneath two oaks. At his destination, he tapped Jesse curtly on the shoulder. "Cutting in."

"This is my dance, Jackson," Jesse informed him mildly. "You'll have to wait your turn."

As Jesse danced her away, Jackson followed, tapping his shoulder again. "Cutting in, Jesse. Now."

"Jackson!" Haley exclaimed. "You're being rude."

"It's all right, Doc. I'll catch another dance later." The cowhand grinned, kissed her forehead, and walked away.

Haley was so angry, she would have followed, but Jackson had made enough of a scene. She wouldn't add to it. When he took her in his arms, falling into the rhythm of the tune, she held herself aloof, struggling for calm. When she could trust herself to speak, she scolded him. "That was ridiculous, you know."

"No. I don't know." His hand strayed down her back and over her side. Beneath her gown, he could feel the heat of her body, the defined prominence of her ribs. She wasn't skinny, or emaciated, but she was thinner. "You're tired, and that pack of panting mongrels hasn't enough brains between them to see it."

"You're saying it's their place to decide if I should or shouldn't dance? And if they don't, you will?" His arrogance made her laugh. "In case you haven't noticed, I'm a grown woman. I decide when I'm too tired, or not. I decide if I dance or not. I decide with whom."

Suddenly Haley stopped. In the middle of the dance, in the middle of the crowded dance floor, she stopped dancing. Looking up at him, a proud, defiant glitter in her eyes. "At the moment, Jackson Cade, I don't want to dance with you."

Abruptly, she left him standing there, his mouth agape as she walked through the crowd and into the inn.

"Uh-oh," Yancey observed from his distant place on the sidelines. "He put his foot in it."

"All the way to his knee," Daniel agreed.

"Do you think he knows?" Cooper was frowning as Jackson weaved through the milling crowd back to them.

"What we're doing? Or that he's head over heels crazy for her?" Jesse asked in a low chuckle.

"Both," Yancey and Coop said in unison.

"On the first, he hasn't a clue," Jesse said. "On the last, he'd going down for the third time and fighting himself, what he feels, and anyone else who gets in his path."

"From the look of him, I don't want it to be me," Cooper decided. "My hands are my life, I can't jeopardize that to perpetuate your little matchmaking scheme, Jesse."

"You won't have to. Once was enough." Yancey knew Jackson better than the surgeon and the conductor, he knew the power contained in that deceptively muscled body. He understood better than anyone except Jesse exactly how carefully the third Cade brother guarded his strength. "Let him play this as he wishes. A little teasing and a joke or two in return can't hurt."

"Just don't let him know we're onto him, or he'll get stubborn on us and this will take months longer."

"Anyone understand what this stubbornness is about?" Daniel, who hadn't grown up in the lowcountry like Yancey and Cooper, lacked their advantage of knowing that the most unyielding of the Cades also never talked his troubles.

"There's only one thing I can guarantee about Jackson Cade." Yancey's laugh was short, wry. "Whatever it is, it happened a long time ago. And only Jackson Cade and God understand."

"And maybe one day the doc," Jesse, who knew him second best, added into the mix.

"Brace yourselves," Cooper warned. "Here he comes."

But Jackson didn't come to confront his friends. He didn't go in search of Haley. Instead, Jericho came to him.

"The break I mentioned regarding River Trace just became reality." Jericho had caught his arm and leaned close. His words were nearly lost in the beat of music.

"You know who nearly killed Dancer." It was a statement, not a question. Jackson knew Jericho wouldn't have spoken as positively if there was any but the most remote doubt.

"I know who has admitted to it." The sheriff, who seemed even more imposing in formal dress than in his always-immaculate uniform, looked grim and not so happy with the news. "I need for you to go downtown with me to verify some of the kid's story."

"A kid?"

"I'm afraid so."

"How old?"

Jericho shook his head sorrowfully. "Fourteen."

"Ah, no!" Jackson had been fourteen when he'd made the mistake of his life. But his was a mistake that hadn't hurt anyone but him. Nor had it affected any lives but his. Until Haley.

"Yeah." Jericho straightened and stared over the heads of the crowd. "I hate it when a minor's involved." His searching gaze found his wife. "I want to speak to Maria, then, if you like, I'll give you a ride downtown to the station."

"No." Jackson, too, was searching the crowd. He, too, found the person he searched for. "You go on when you're ready. If I'm not there before you, I won't be far behind."

A nod from Jericho and he was gone, moving through the crowd to Maria. Jackson did an about-face. Intent on following Haley, he left the gala and the public part of the garden behind.

The garden sprawled over acres, and Cullen's restoration of each section was nothing short of magical. Most of it was intended for the pleasure of guests of the inn. But a gated section surrounding the River Cottage had always been kept apart. Once the cottage had been lodgings for special guests in need of absolute privacy. Now it was Eden and Adams's home.

As he slipped past the gate that was never locked, and walked the dimly lighted path, Jackson saw Haley sitting in the gazebo perched on a tiny island bordered by a small creek and the broadest part of the unromantically named Broad River. Her head was down. Her shoulders didn't slump, but something about their determined set told him only a great effort prevented it.

Moonlight streamed across the water, catching in ripples as the tide rose. Away from the lights and laughter of the party the world was silver and midnight blue, and Haley sat in silence in the darkness of the charming, secluded structure.

His footsteps sounded on the wooden boardwalk crossing the creek. He made no effort to quiet them, for he didn't want to frighten her as he had before. If Haley heard, she didn't react.

The soil of the tiny spit of land was loamy and damp. Wild ferns and wildflowers grew in profusion around the gazebo. The path that led from the boardwalk was a scattering of shells that gleamed like alabaster in the light of the night and crackled under his feet with each step. And still she didn't move.

"Haley," he called her name softly. Another warning so she would know it was he who approached, not a monster. She took a deep breath, almost a sigh, and said nothing. "Duchess."

She laughed softly then. Ruefully. Bitterly.

Bitterly. An emotion he'd never associated with her. Haley had never seemed to harbor bitterness for anything. Not even the scars, he suspected. She simply accepted that the world and its people were as they were, and bitterness couldn't change it. So she coped, and transcending enmity and spite, moved on with her life and her life's work.

She was a woman beyond his scope. A woman he didn't understand, especially her feelings. And now he couldn't understand his own. He was a juggernaut with vacillating emotions, running roughshod over any who disturbed him.

No, he corrected. Not over just anyone. Over Haley.

"Duchess," Haley said, speaking at last. "That single word says it all, doesn't it?"

"I don't understand." He stood at the steps of the gazebo. He wanted to go to her, but he knew she would rebuff him. Perhaps cringe from his touch in disgust. He couldn't bear it if she cringed. "It's just a name."

"A name?" She was a profile shaped by the gleam of the ruffled river, her every move scored on his mind and heart in silver and blue-black. Her hands had been resting in her lap, now she clasped them together, palm to palm, the fingers of one folding over the back of the other, as if she needed to calm their trembling. Still, she didn't turn to him. "I would call it a weapon. A very effective weapon. One to keep the enemy terribly off balance. One minute cruel, mocking, and cold. The next..."

She didn't finish the thought. She didn't move. Nor did Jackson. He couldn't. He didn't speak. What was there to say? She was right, the name had begun as a mocking insult. And yes, he'd been cold, but less hate*ful* than he'd been hate-*filled*. Now he knew there was nothing to mock, nothing deserving insults. He'd finally realized his hatred was the result of one woman's influence, his mother's, and should be reserved for her alone.

Now, in this minute, with the moon as his dawning light, what he felt for Haley, for the Duchess, was far from cold, far from mockery. Far from hate.

"I didn't mean to hurt you." He spoke into a silence broken only by the river whispering over the shore and by the songs of creatures of the night. "Someone, yes. But not you. I'm a slow learner, it took me a while to realize that."

"So, with this great realization you come barreling into my life, as if you own it and me. As if you care. *This* time." She turned then to look at him. Or, perhaps, at the shape he cast against the moonlit scene behind him. "What will it be tomorrow, or the day after? Or next week? Which way will the seesaw swing?

"I've done this before, Jackson. With a man who was two people. I discovered too late, he could be kinder than kind, and in the next breath unspeakably cruel. I won't relive it."

"The man from your past." One of the crazed creatures she'd spoken of facing. The comparison hurt. "He branded you."

"Yes. Todd did that."

She didn't act coy, or ask how he knew. She would remember the night in the barn and its aftermath.

"Where is he now?"

"Does it matter, Jackson?"

"To me it does."

"Why?"

"Because I'd like to throttle him with my bare hands."

She sighed, a sad sound. "You would, wouldn't you?"

"I want it more than anything." *Except to hold her and erase the cruel memories from her mind.* But he couldn't say that. He'd lost the right to say it. "Do you believe me?"

"In that, yes. I do."

"Who was this Todd, Haley? Where is he?" Jackson couldn't leave it alone. The monster needed a name.

"Todd Flynn was my husband. I took back my own name after the divorce. He's in prison now."

"How long?" Jackson's words were strangled. His voice strained. "For how long did the system lock the bastard away?"

"On a number of charges, for a number of years, contingent on behavior. I'm to be notified when he's released."

Jackson considered the sort of man she described. He'd crossed paths with men of Todd's ilk too many times. They were slime, snakes who walked, treacherous charmers. Men with one false face, one real. The false hiding the truth. They were, without fail, obsessive. Obsessive in their charm. Obsessive in the need to control. Obsessively possessive and dangerously unstable.

Rage rose in him. Rage meant for a brutal stranger.

"Haley." Her name was a raw sound on his tongue. "I would never hurt you as he did. I couldn't."

Her head had bowed again. Now it came up, her gaze seeking him in the dark of a cloud that had passed over the moon. "For all your faults, I know that, Jackson. Probably better than you. I had two years to learn from Todd which sort would."

"Two?" The time span shook him. "You stayed two years?"

"Almost. His behavior was a slow downward spiral. Too innocuous at first to recognize. He didn't like his job, then an accident left him with a problem. I thought the change was a combination of dissatisfaction and a sort of grief. I hoped counseling would help. He refused. Matters grew worse. He became more and more controlling and suspicious, and finally combative.''

"He hit you."

"Just once. And I left. The cigarette burns came later, punishment for the divorce.''

She fell silent again. Jackson waited, not sure what he should say. So he left it to Haley to speak. When she did, it wasn't what he wanted to hear.

"Go away, Jackson. You're right, I'm tired. My head hurts from trying to figure you out. Just go. Please.''

Jackson said nothing more. After a time he turned from her. Ferns stirred, shells crackled beneath his feet. Next came the hollow sound of steps on the boardwalk. Each fading a little more. Fading until the night surrounding Haley was quiet, but for the wash of the tide and night creatures.

Then she cried. A strong woman's silent tears of grief.

Eight

She was tall and gaunt, emaciated. Her dark hair, streaked with silver, was drawn back from a deeply creased forehead by plastic combs. The heavy fall from the combs was gathered in a tight coil held by a dagger-like pin that could only be silver. Her dress was faded, scrupulously clean, starched and neatly pressed. Beyond the silver pin and a narrow band on one finger, her only adornment was a collar of handmade lace. She sat perfectly erect, her back never touching the chair. No board could be more straight.

Hands folded in her lap, she didn't fuss or fidget for having to wait. She simply sat calmly. A woman of learned patience. A woman of strength and principles.

A boy lounged by her side. His back was not straight, his hands were not still. Beneath a shock of hair, his eyes darted, his petulant mouth curled in resentment. His clothes, true to current and unkempt style, were as clean as the old woman's.

Jackson watched them through the glass door of Jericho's

office. He hadn't known what to expect when he left the inn and the gala, but it would never have been this woman.

He looked to Jericho. "She brought him in?"

"An hour ago, according to Court Hamilton, who drew the short straw." At Jackson's puzzled look, he explained, "Drawing the short straw meant Court would hold down the fort instead of attending Eden's party."

"Tough."

"Not so tough—he'll be exempt from the draw for a few months." Jericho chuckled. "Not exactly professional, but it works, and fairly, for a small department."

Jericho didn't say it, but Jackson knew he'd drawn a straw. "What counts is that it works."

"This time to best advantage. Of the staff, Court is the least prejudiced toward the Rabbs."

Jackson stared through the door. "The woman's a Rabb?"

"The mother of the lot of them."

"The boy shared his drugs with Dancer?" In body and size, the boy looked fourteen. His face and attitude were much older. Life was hard in Rabb Town. The children grew up fast. The women aged even faster. "She isn't his grandmother."

"No," Jericho said, his thoughts paralleling Jackson's. "The Rabbs breed early and long. The kid is a late child, but she isn't as old as she looks."

"She's the one who called. The telephone tip." Jackson watched her still, quiet hands. No nonsense, work-worn hands. Chapped, short nails, but like her clothing, scrupulously clean. A poor woman. Rabb men were never good providers. Moonshiners, brawlers, prolific breeders, but never conscientious family men.

"Why is she here?" Jackson questioned. "After all the years of enmity between the Rabbs and the rest of the world, especially the Cades, why now?"

"It has to do with the boy. And that for the first time in her life, Daisy Rabb has the support of a friend." Booted footsteps rang hollowly on the bare, uncarpeted floor as Jericho crossed to his desk. Taking a folder from a neat stack of papers, he returned to the door. "Take a look at these."

The folder was fat and heavy. If it was a file of the boy's offenses, it would be a long one for such a young child. Expecting to have a wealth of reading to do, Jackson sat down in the nearest chair and laid the file on a table beside it.

When he opened it, he did not discover the sordid criminal history of a juvenile. Instead, it was filled with exquisitely detailed drawings of the wildlife and flowers found in the marshes and swamps of the lowcountry.

He caught a startled breath. "The boy did this?"

"Yes. He's only fourteen, he's never had a lesson of even a minute of instruction, and—other than his mother—no encouragement." Jericho leaned over Jackson's shoulder to pick up a drawing of an owl that looked as if at any time it might blink and swivel its head. "And he can do this."

"The same kid who nearly killed Dancer."

"So it seems." Jericho shuffled through the drawings for a certain one that would confuse the point more. When he found it, he laid it at the top of the stack, saying no more.

The other work had been single scenes of creatures in natural habitats. This was two scenes. The first of a puppy caught in a trap, its mother standing guard. In the second, the puppy was lifeless, its starving mother still standing guard.

The love and compassion were almost palpable. Emotions the artist would have to feel to paint them so clearly.

"And he nearly destroyed Dancer," Jackson repeated in a baffled tone. "It makes no sense."

"Maybe it does, Jackson, when you remember his brothers. When you consider how they would feel with a baby brother half their age who would rather draw than fight."

"You think he was goaded into coming to River Trace?"

"Goaded and brainwashed." The sheriff selected another drawing, one of a hummingbird perched on a water lily. "Made to think he was less of man because he created beauty rather than destroyed it. Made to believe he must become a destroyer to prove something he didn't want to prove."

Laying the drawing aside, Jericho's face turned grim. "The boy feels he's failed in some way. I'm afraid he's going to go too far the other way. So is his mother."

"Like Junior," Jackson mused. "Trying to kill Adams."

"And Snake, a younger version of Junior. Maybe worse. The saving grace may be that there are six fairly decent sisters in between. The sisters, his art, his mother, and Haley."

Jackson didn't react or look away from the drawings. When he did, utter confusion was written on his face. "Haley?" Worry lined his face. "How does she figure in this?"

"Haley persuaded Daisy Rabb to bring the boy in."

"Why would she do this?" Jackson left his chair to go to the door. Through the glass he studied the woman and the boy. She still hadn't moved. He was still sullen. "How did Haley meet a Rabb in the first place?"

A shiver of fear raced down his spine as Jackson realized it wasn't beyond the scope of possibilities that Snake Rabb would hurt her for no other reason than that she was in partnership with a Cade. "Surely she hasn't been to Rabb Town?"

"As a matter of fact, she has."

Jackson turned from his study of the woman and the boy, horror written on his face. "Haley went to treat an animal in a place that's little better than a sadistic slaughterhouse?"

"She went for the boy."

"Of course," Jackson drawled. "That's clear as mud. Why didn't I think of it? Out of curiosity, not because it enhances this wild tale even a little, does this kid have a name?"

"His name is John. Haley calls him Johnny."

"Ah." The word was a low growl. "Haley again. This begins to sound like a story I should hear."

"That's why you're here. I want you to hear it from the boy and his mother. I'd intended asking Haley, but it was clear you were quarreling. Added to that, she's had a hard week. If she's slept three hours a night in the last six nights, I'll be surprised. So it's just the four of us."

"Why now?" Jackson moved to a window, looking out at the night and the streets of Belle Terre. Old-fashioned gaslights, carefully preserved, flickered along the narrow thoroughfare, their glow broken by a modern electric light only here and there. The historic ambience of the city had been meticulously perpetuated. So had the rancor. "Why did this woman choose this night, or any night? Why not in daylight like normal citizens?"

"Because she isn't guided by normal rules. Daisy Rabb must do what she can do, when she can." Before Jackson could comment, Jericho explained with the patience he would use with a child, "Think about it. Junior's in prison, but Snake is very much present. What would he do if he knew she was coming and bringing Johnny in to confess?"

"Even though she's his mother, that doesn't bear considering," Jackson admitted, turning his back on the view of the peaceful streets of Belle Terre. "So she had to seize the moment and the opportunity when she could. Morning or midnight, or whenever. A time when Snake wasn't around.

"Where is he tonight, Jericho? Poaching deer? Dropping a stick or two of dynamite in a fish pond? Setting an illegal trap, which he will take up later and throw in a creek without disarming it, so an unsuspecting five-year-old can nearly lose a leg to it?"

"Lincoln's son is all right now, Jackson," Jericho said mildly, hiding his own anger over the injury young Cade sustained. "We don't know it was Snake's trap."

"What you mean, Jericho, is we can't prove it was his trap. But as sure as there's salt in the sea, we know it was his."

Jericho had begun to despair for the success of this evening and for Haley's plan. Now, Jackson's attachment and love for Lincoln's young son, gave him the leverage he needed. "What if Cade were in a place and a situation like Johnny Rabb?"

"He isn't. His mother would never allow it."

"But if he were," Jericho countered with more of the monumental patience that made him the distinguished sheriff he was. "What would you want for him? For Cade?"

"I would want someone to help him." Jackson's gaze was vague, seeing the squalor of Rabb Town and the coarseness of its denizens as the environment of a boy like Cade. Softly, in a near whisper, he murmured, "I'd hope someone would help him."

"Yeah," Jericho agreed. "Just as I hope someone will help Johnny Rabb. I'm going to take Mrs. Rabb and the boy into the lounge, where she'll be more comfortable. Give me a few minutes to get the necessary paperwork out of the way, then join us.

"While you wait—" the massive man, the most gentle of men, took a second folder from his desk "—take a look at these."

Jericho was gone before Jackson opened the second folder. The compassionate sheriff of Belle Terre had led the gaunt, weary woman with patience learned of fear, and the sullen boy poised on the brink of disaster, to a quieter, more comfortable place before Jackson realized exactly what he was seeing.

The folder held drawings of horses, each so perfect a camera couldn't have been more accurate. But these were better than photographs. For they were done with care and love.

They were Jackson's horses. He could recognize and name each one. Extraordinary talent had created breathtaking likenesses. Johnny Rabb, a boy who loved horses and expressed it in his work. A boy and talent worth saving.

As he closed the folder, Jackson knew he'd been manipulated by a master. Touché, Jericho. But it didn't matter. When a man was as stubborn as the hellion of the Cades, Jackson supposed that for a good cause, the end truly justified the means.

Filled with regret for the troubles of the innocents, he went to speak with a downtrodden woman and the gifted boy who was her hope, and the hope of the Rabbs, for a better future.

Pausing at the door of the lounge, he envisioned Haley, another woman who'd made the best of a terrible situation. He prayed she had someone who had helped. Turning the knob, he opened the door and stepped in. With his hand outstretched, he went to the gaunt woman he realized now was old even by the day's standards to have a child as young as Johnny, yet not as aged as he had thought.

Daisy Rabb had been a beautiful woman before the ravages of time and hardship had taken their toll. Traces of that beauty still lingered in ways neither misfortune nor years could take from her. Beneath a wrinkled and sallow complexion lay a strong bone structure that was the hallmark of enduring character. Eyes a softer brown than her son's held a look of unbending pride that upheld the strength of principles when her world deteriorated into the squalor of Rabb Town.

There was intelligence in her eyes. Intelligence and pride and love. Love for the son who was different. Her dream for the future. Perhaps her reason for living. Her salvation.

In another time, another era, women did not speak the shame they considered their lot to bear. They didn't speak of hardships. They didn't speak of abuse. Bound by vows they would not abandon, they endured. Some withered away in mind, body, and spirit. Some grew stronger. Which in the end, could be the hardest road.

Daisy Rabb was one of the strong ones. She had paid the cost. She was here tonight determined a part of that cost wouldn't be her last child. Her youngest son.

Jackson knew then he could not refuse her desperate need. Taking her rough hand, meeting her weary gaze, he said, "Mrs. Rabb, I'm Jackson Cade, and I've come to help."

But for the gaslight by the heavy wrought-iron gate, the night was like a great dark cave. Clouds that threatened the moon hours before had gathered and thickened, hiding the sky. For a while, a scattering of stars was still visible, shining out of relentless darkness like the hope Jackson had seen in the eyes of a desperate mother.

Now, the last of the stars was gone, lost behind the lowering cloud cover. Lightning flashed in jagged lines across the horizon. Distant thunder sounded and sounded again like the rumble of carriage wheels over cobblestones. By morning the ever-thirsty earth of the lowcountry would feel the lash of rain.

As Jackson felt the lash of regret. Regret that had drawn him here, to the locked and bolted gate of the little house at Seventeen Jessamine Street. Reading the scrolled and ornate metal placard set in the tabby of the garden walls more than a century ago, a small smile lifted the corners of his mouth.

"Jessamine." With a finger he traced the proper name for the flower for which the street had been named. "Jasmine," he said again, sounding the S as if it were the double Z, as any born-and-bred or acclimatized lowcountryman would say it. "Jazzmine."

The small cul-de-sac was quiet. Only a few houses lined the narrow street and the tightly curling circle. Except for their narrow street facade, those few and the lives they sheltered were as hidden from view by gardens and walls as Seventeen Jessamine. At little more than three hours before dawn, no prying eyes peered through lace curtains at the man who paced the street.

No telephone receivers were lifted to summon one of Jericho's faultlessly uniformed guardians of the night to drive the loiterer away. For that, Jericho's unknowing brigade should be thankful. For leaving his self-assigned post was not part of Jackson Cade's resolute purpose.

He had stopped pacing and hunkered down on the steps of the little-used street entrance of the house, when a flash of lights preceded the hum of the engine of a slow-moving automobile. Almost immediately Jesse Lee's truck came into view.

Though the truck was old and had seen long and hard use at Belle Reve and River Trace, it was clean and well cared for. As all Jesse Lee's rides were cared for, whether old or new or young, mechanical or four-legged.

Jackson waited in the shadow of the small porch until the truck came to a halt by the curb near the courtyard gate. He waited until the light triggered by Jesse's opened door illuminated the interior of the truck. He watched as the older man crossed to the passenger side. By the time that second door had opened, he was there, standing shoulder to shoulder with Jesse, saying in a husky voice, "I'll take her."

Showing no surprise at finding Jackson Cade waiting on the secluded street at only a little before dawn, Jesse only nodded and stepped aside.

Haley was sleeping, half curled, half sitting in the worn seat. She should have seemed out of place there in her flame silk dress, but Jackson was discovering that with this woman there were no pretensions. However she was dressed, wherever she went, she was simply Haley Garrett. No more, and certainly no less, than the strong, caring woman he hadn't believed she could be.

"She's exhausted." Jesse spoke at last as Jackson lifted her into his arms and turned from the truck. "Falling asleep like this in my truck will embarrass her."

"No." Jackson shook his head, aware that Jesse was warning him off. Warning that there must be no mockery this night. "She won't be embarrassed. I won't let her be."

"You quarreled with her before." The cowhand wasn't quite ready to let his worry go.

"I won't anymore."

Jesse's faded look held Jackson's, as in the gloom he read the truth of that promise on the younger face. A single, sharp tilt of his head, a move less keenly interested eyes might have missed, signaled his final surrender of his cherished cargo. His date for the evening.

Saying no more, realizing no other admonitions were needed, Jesse opened the gate. He followed Jackson through the courtyard and fragrant garden. Producing a key, he opened the door to the tiny house and stepped aside.

Jackson paused as he looked back, old and young eyes meeting again over Haley's head as it nestled in the curve of his throat and his shoulder. It was the look of two men who loved the same woman. One like a daughter and a friend. The other...

Jackson wasn't sure how he loved her. How he would be *allowed* to love her. Beloved enemy? Friend? Lover? Mate?

He knew he deserved neither of the last two. But, at last, he understood which he wanted.

The moment passed, Jesse nodded again. The same curt, decisive gesture. Jackson turned away and didn't look back as he crossed the room and mounted the stairs that led to the bedroom with a balcony that overlooked the garden. The barely audible sound of his footsteps faded completely before Jesse pulled the door closed and turned away himself.

Moving quietly through shadows cloistering the edges of the courtyard, he went to the street. Pausing there by the open gate, he looked up, waiting. In the darkened room he supposed was her bedroom, suddenly a light gleamed through a small window of lead and antique glass, casting patterns on the ribbon of lawn below.

Jesse stood as he was, listening to a silence only enhanced by the splash to an aged fountain. He stood, he listened, he watched, until the light from the small window was extinguished. Until the patterns no longer lay on green grass. Only then did he step through the gate, close it, and return to his truck.

"Good luck," he said as lightning streaked across the far sky once again, leaving its jagged memory etched in his sight. When the engine rumbled to life, with one last wish for wisdom, he set the proper gear. "Good luck." His words seemed to hang in the air, waiting. "To both of you."

Thunder rolled in answer to the lightning. The storm was still miles and miles in the distance as, without looking back, Jesse Lee drove away from Jessamine Street.

The minute he was oriented, with the arrangement of Haley's bedroom forever imprinted in his mind, Jackson flicked off the light. Guided by memory and a small night-light burning on a bedside table, he carried her to her bed. Sitting with her on its edge, he eased her from his lap. Holding her with one arm and one hand, he slipped his free hand beneath a pillow. As he hoped, his fingers skimmed over a folded scrap of fabric he knew must be the garment she'd laid out for the night.

In the darkness, in the stillness, his sense of awareness was heightened. The smooth fabric of the gown felt like Haley. Soft, smooth, with a hint of roughness in the lace of the bodice, like the feel of her skin. Vexing and provocative, maddening.

The room looked like Haley. Spare, utilitarian, with classic touches that made it unique. It smelled like her. Like her skin, her hair, her clothing. Crisp, clean, and blended with it the pleasant scent of jasmine.

Sparing a thought to how appropriate it was she wore the scent for which the street was named, he tried to shut his mind to all else. He was here to see that she slept and rested for as long as she could. He was here to watch over her—then, when she was ready to listen, to apologize and explain.

Sleep, rest, apology, explanation, in that order. Then he would go home to River Trace. The seduction of his senses or of Haley was not part of his plan.

Shaking the nightgown free of its folds, discovering it was every bit as tempting as he feared, and more, he steeled himself by muttering the litany of his resolve again. "Sleep, rest, apology, explanation."

"Hmm?" she murmured and snuggled back against him.

"It was nothing, love," he assured her, even though he knew she had no idea he was here, and certainly not what he said. "We just need to get you out of this gown and into the other one."

She stirred, nestling against him, but only as a sleeper might seek a more comfortable position without waking. Her hair brushed his cheek. He was distracted by jasmine—by the room, the nightgown, her hair—each whispering of the intriguing, tantalizing fragrance. Steeling himself against baser instincts that clamored louder by the minute, he slid his hand down her back, searching for the zipper he knew such a slender gown would require.

She was so soft, so sweet, the sleek fabric slid beneath his hand so temptingly, that by the time the zipper was drawn down, his teeth were clenched so tightly they were at risk. Discovering that she wore no more than panties beneath the gown only added fuel to the inferno.

"I can do this." The words were half snarl, half prayer. "And I can do it as a gentleman. God willing."

He realized there was no help for it, but simply to do what was needed. Sliding the gown from her shoulders, his cuff caught on the tiny buttons at the front and throat. Which required that he look where he never intended to look.

In the little light her bared breasts were dusky, their crests only a little darker, and so tempting. He longed to feel their softness against his lips, to wrap his tongue around the budlike tips and tug it into his mouth. He wanted…

"Jackson, what are you doing?"

Lifting his gaze from her breasts, he found Haley watching him. Her eyes were heavy-lidded, the look in them confused, unfocused. With a little shake of her head, she smiled wanly. "I thought I dreamed you. You were holding me as if you cared, as if I were precious, and I knew it could only be a dream."

A puzzled frown crossed her face. "But you're here." The frown deepened as she looked around the room. "Jesse. Where's Jesse? He was bringing me home."

"Jesse did drive you home, Duchess. But he's gone now."

"Gone? Why? I was going to offer him a cup of coffee. Jesse loves coffee."

"Yes, he does," Jackson agreed. He would have agreed to anything to get through this. "But he's gone back to River Trace. Straighten your arms, just a bit," he said without a change of tone, as if he discussed another man while he helped a beautiful woman undress every day of his life. In a hurried move he slipped the dress away. Haley didn't seem to notice or care that she was nearly naked in his arms.

"Why?" She moved again, her bare flesh cool against his heated skin. Her breasts and the nipples he wanted to kiss and caress but dared not seemed to sear his chest.

Jackson lost the thread of her conversation.

"Why did Jesse leave?"

"You were asleep when you arrived. Here, love, lift your arms." When she obeyed without question, he slipped the gown down her body. It pooled in glittering folds at her hips. Pretending this was no more than the sort of random bedtime chatter he participated in when he visited Lincoln and Linsey and put Cade to bed, he returned to his explanation. "Jesse left because I told him I would take care of you."

"You were waiting for us."

She was awake now. Jackson realized she'd been fully awake for sometime. Likely from the moment he lifted her from Jesse's car. Payback. Putting him through his paces. Collecting her pound of revenge. Whatever she wanted to call it, after this evening and the weeks that had gone before, he deserved it.

"I was waiting by the courtyard gate when you arrived."

In a flash of lightning, her eyes shone blue fire. The ivory and pale beige of her gown seemed to scintillate, catching latent electricity that crackled between them. If her bare breasts were provocative, with taunting lace cupping the perfect shape and playing hide and seek with nipples tightened and darkened like dusky pearls, they were mesmerizing.

That the touch of his eyes affected her should have given him some satisfaction. It only drove him crazier.

"Will you tell me why, Jackson?"

"I came to apologize. For everything. And especially for tonight. I meddled in your life and I had no right."

"Because you knew I was tired and you felt I should rest?" Haley stood, and with her hands she smoothed the long skirt of the gown down her body and over her hips. Walking to the French doors, she flung them open and stepped onto the balcony. The storm was still a distant threat, but the breeze it drove before it brushed over her, teasing tendrils from the coil of her hair, molding the gown even more closely about her.

Lifting her face to the unrelenting darkness of the cloud-shrouded sky, she stood for the time of a long breath, considering what she was about to do. Then, realizing there was nothing to consider, she swung around. Leaning against the balcony railing, with her arms folded beneath her breasts, she looked into the eyes of the man she had loved too long from afar.

It was time she took control of her life again. Time Jackson Cade learned a lesson and understood the rules of the game of loving and being loved. But that she would leave for tomorrow.

"There was another reason you were angry with your friends tonight," she said, so very softly he barely heard. "Or am I mistaken?"

"There was another reason." His hands were tight fists, against the need to know the heat and contour of her body under the gliding journey of his plundering, seeking palms.

Leaving the balcony, she moved to the doorway. In the tiny illumination of the night-light the ivory of her gown became silver, the beige, gold. The slender straps were little more than threads, the lace covering her breasts, scant. In a night that had grown sultry in the presage of changing weather, silk clung closer, revealed more.

Her voice was husky, breaking the little silence. "Will you tell me, Jackson?"

He could not have refused her anything in this moment, and he'd come to be honest. "I was disturbed because I didn't want Daniel, or Cooper, or Yancey, or even Jesse, touching you. I was angry because I was jealous."

"Because you want me." She asked no question.

"Yes."

"You want me, but you didn't come to make love to me."

"I didn't come to make love to you, Haley."

Lifting her arms, letting the scraps of lace covering her breasts slip until they barely covered her, she plucked the ebony and pearl stylus from her hair. A shake of her head sent the tousled mane tumbling to her shoulders in a fall of sparkling silver and muted gold.

In that startling moment, she looked as if she'd just risen

from her lover's bed. Jackson could only watch as she walked toward him as if she had all the time in the world. When she stopped before him, her body nearly touching his, it took all his strength not to reach for her.

"Why did you come so determined that you wouldn't make love to me?" A fingertip traced the line of a tuck in his shirt. An innocent act that in this setting was anything but innocent.

Jackson held himself ramrod-straight. One little bend in his resolve and he would be lost. "For once in my life, for you, I wanted to do the right thing."

"For me."

"For you."

"And if I want you? Here, now, with no apologies, no promises? Just for the night, with no regard for tomorrow? What then, Jackson Cade?"

Jackson took a step back. "A few hours ago you were angry with me. Too angry for this."

Haley nodded. "I was angry with the man you were a few hours ago. That man wouldn't have come here tonight. He wouldn't have admitted he cared enough to be jealous. He wouldn't have fought so hard against this."

Rising on tiptoe, she skimmed his lips with hers. Once, twice, then again, teasing, making love with her kiss.

"Duchess," he whispered against her seducing mouth. "This can't be what you want. You don't know what you're doing."

Laughing, she drew him closer. "Ah, yes, I do. Better than you, Jackson Cade. I've known I wanted this since I was fifteen."

Nine

"Jackson."

His name was a whisper. She'd meant to tease, to laugh a little as if this were a game. But what she saw in his eyes swept the words away, leaving her with only his name.

With her palm she cupped his cheek. Fingertips barely dancing over the lightly bearded line of his jaw, with her touch she sought his mouth. His hard, grim mouth that could soften into a heart-stopping smile. Or a kiss.

A kiss. She needed his kiss, here, now, more than she needed breath. More than she needed anything but Jackson. Dancing fingers lingered, then glided away from his lips to his throat, then to his nape. As she rose on tiptoe to take what she needed so shockingly, she drew him down to her.

Jackson didn't resist. Though his mouth yielded to hers, he didn't move as with her kiss she proved his every bitterly held prejudice a lie. As if it were a power beyond his scope, the delicate and elusive touch of her tongue against his sealed lips stripped away the protective bias he'd worn like a shield. A shield shattering with every touch.

With it went the honor that kept him from reaching for her. Crumbling honor too weak to deter him from making love to her. As, he admitted now, he'd wanted to do since the night she'd come to River Trace and slept in his bed. As he'd known from his first glimpse of her that the day would come when he would want and even need Haley Garrett.

As he wanted her now, and honor be damned—if proof that she'd been hurt too much already didn't loom in stark horror in his mind. With his hands curling over her shoulders, trying to ignore the feel of her against his palms, he put her from him. "No, Duchess. This can't be."

With a harsh shake of his head, he released her and backed away. Not daring to meet her eyes, he remembered the night and the gala, and that she'd asked him to go away. "You're tired and groggy and dazed from sleep. You don't know..."

"What I'm doing?" she finished for him with a low laugh. "Ah, Jackson, don't you know that I was awake the minute you touched me? Don't you know that I realize what it cost you to come here tonight and what it means? Don't you know that what I see in your eyes is the look I've dreamed of since I was fifteen?"

Fifteen? Even as a questioning frown flickered over his face, she saw the need for an answer was lost as quickly in a blaze of stronger need. As his gaze swept over her filled with the passion of her dreams once more, touching his cheek again, she smiled serenely. "I'm not dazed, or tired. I've never felt more alive than I do now. And I've never been surer of what I want.

"I want you, Jackson Cade—warts, temper, stubbornness and all, I want you." Stepping into the small, pale illumination cast by the night-light, with her hair flowing down her back like a river of rich gold and the thrust of her breasts turning lace to gossamer, she stood calmly before him. "If that shocks you, I'm sorry. But not for myself, for you.

"Who knows where tonight may lead? I have no crystal

ball. I can't read tea leaves. But I learned long ago that life didn't come with guarantees. I've made mistakes, I've been disappointed, and I've been hurt. I survived. I will again.

"When you came to me tonight, I thought…" A long breath sounded like a sigh, lace slipped. "Another misjudgment." In a gamble, and with a prayer, a blue gaze as dark as the predawn sky held his. "You really don't want me after all, do you, Jackson?"

"No." The word was a low, rumbled growl.

Haley bowed her head. She stood silently before him. Neither of them moved. Neither spoke. In a soft rustle of leaves a breeze stirred and drifted through the open door, ruffling the pages of an open book and tangling in her hair. A single lock of gold brushed her cheek like flyaway silk. As her scent, the scent of jasmine, enfolded him, he reached out for the errant strand, intending to brush it away. The graze of his fingertips against her cheek brought a sigh as she raised her gaze to meet his.

The color had drained from her face. Even in the faint luminescence, her pallor was evident. Yet she held his stare, keeping it for a silent moment as his hand fell away. With a barely perceptible shrug of her shoulders, as she turned from him, in a whisper she gambled again. "My mistake."

"No." Even Jackson wasn't cognizant of what he was saying. As he brought her back to him, all he knew was that lately no meant yes and yes meant no when Haley Garret was concerned.

"No," he muttered again, but not because his head had cleared. "No, you didn't make a mistake. And no, I shouldn't be doing this. Dammit! I vowed I *wouldn't* do this."

As she threw back her head to stare up at him, his own head dipped. His mouth grazed hers gently as he whispered, "But I am."

Then his hunger wasn't gentle anymore. He crushed her hard against him, molding her body to his. His kiss deepened, a revelation of the power of his desire. Filling his hands with her hair, he made love with teasing lips and caressing tongue.

"Wait." A command, a plea, the word rumbled in his throat as he backed away the space needed to divest himself of jacket and shirt. Then, not able to bear even that small separation, he brought her back to him. Back where she belonged.

Only a wisp of lace lay between them, but it was too much. He wanted to see her, all of her. He wanted to feel the bare heat of her flesh against his own. Winding his fingers through the fall of her hair as before, he tugged back her head again, kissing his way down her throat and across one shoulder. Once there, hooking a finger beneath each strap of her gown, he slipped them down.

The garment caught between them. A subtle shift of her arms and body sent it gliding to the floor. But for a charming trifle of lace panties, Haley was naked, and in his arms again. She shivered and a husky moan met his kiss in response to the skim of his hands down the sides of her breasts and ribs to her hips.

With the thrust of his aroused body sending shards of longing surging through her, she had to know. "No mistake?"

"No mistake." If the assurance of his words hadn't been enough, their tone, the hoarseness in his voice, would have served.

"Then as handsome as you are in formal wear, you have on far too many clothes for this occasion." It was Haley who found the zipper of his trousers and stepped away as he discarded the garments she found offensive.

"You're beautiful," she said when he stood before her completely naked, at last.

"I think that's my line, Duchess." He laughed, letting the fingers of each hand trail from her shoulders to her breasts. The nipples that had taunted him through their veil of lace, were taut and tempting, beguiling in the hollow of his palm. But this time his need didn't demand that he bring her back to him. Instead he kept his distance, watching her and the building of her desire while he traced excruciatingly deliberate and gentle circles around and around the enticing tips.

He was no stranger to a woman's body. He wasn't a monk,

and there had been lovers. Though not so many as one might expect. Jackson liked women, women liked him. Women who were beautiful in their own right, in their own fashion. Women who wanted and expected no more from him than he from them. But to Jackson, none had ever been as lovely, as exciting. None ever made him ache in just this way. "You are, you know. At this moment, you're the most beautiful creature I've ever seen."

"I'm glad." Haley was too honest to lie, even in the sweet agony of passion. "I want to be beautiful for you."

If the last wall of resistance had not already been thoroughly breached, it would have been then. With no thought to old prejudices or to promises a callow boy had made to himself, he caught her up in his arms. As nipples his touch turned to pearls brushed his bare chest, he bent to kiss her.

A kiss too passionate, too needful, to be tender. But neither Haley nor Jackson wanted tenderness. In silent consensus, both knew there would be a quiet time for the softer side of loving. But not now. Not in the chaos of crashing walls and emotions too intense, discovery too new. Too consuming.

As he took her to bed, there were no rules, no history. Neither had gone where they were going together. No one felt as they felt. Or loved as they loved. Jackson, the wild child, the hothead, the strong man, trembled as he touched her learning the contour of her face, then her body.

Her low sigh when he suckled at her breast robbed him of breath, stealing his heart from his body. But it didn't matter. Nothing mattered as his exploring caress trailed over her breasts, her midriff, and down. Down to the brand of another man. The flower of scars lying beneath the prominent bone of her hip, revealed with the discarding of her last concealing garment.

For five petals there were Jackson's five kisses, taking the horror from them. Taking the remembered pain for his own as she had taken his heart. With deepening passion restive and fierce, he understood the strength of a woman who met enmity with quiet dignity, insolence with unfailing courtesy. A woman who conquered with grace and compassion. A woman who walked in honor.

As he rose over her, compelled by desire to wait no longer in making this strong woman his woman, in her touch and in her kiss he found that grace, that compassion, that honor. Each her gift to him, bound with passion as deep and restive as his own. With desire as compelling.

"Duchess," he cried against the tender flesh of her breasts, then again as his mouth took hers, cherishing with his possession. Seducing with the plundering stroke of his tongue. As he sank deeper into her welcoming embrace, his body joining with hers, enfolded at last by hers, he knew he would not give back her pain, or take back his heart.

Haley drowsed and woke. In each waking she found new joy in his lovemaking. Each time she found him the same incredible lover. Yet each time he changed, as needs changed. As she changed.

He was never less possessive, never less provocative, yet impatient passion became patient. Fierce kisses grew tender, urgent. His seeking strokes, protracted, gently drawn, and wonderfully wicked. Each time she thought she couldn't want him more, she discovered she was mistaken. Haley Garrett was not a woman of great experience, but she needed no experience to understand that in the physical act of loving Jackson Cade and being loved in return, there would always be more.

He proved to her that passion, like courage and strength, was never static. As a touch and a kiss changed, so did her response. So did Jackson's, as he taught her the power of her touch, her kiss. Power that made her laugh softly in the joy of being a woman. A sound that to her lover and teacher was sweet music. Even as she reveled in a kiss that made him breathless, in an intimate caress that drew hungry shudders, taking him to the brink of need. It was then she laughed again, and he dragged her back to his arms, wreaking vengeance for her teasing. The delightful vengeance she was seeking. Her teacher's reward.

Beyond the open doors, beyond the balcony, beyond the wall of the garden it overlooked, dawn had come and gone. As the day began for the rest of the world, her body gleaming with the fading heat of sated desire, Haley fell silent and still. In the quiet euphoria of the knowledge that the gift of a lover's joy was hers to give as well as to receive, she slept at last.

Afraid he would wake her, Jackson lay watching her sleep. Watching and wondering. As morning crept by, realizing how deeply she slept, he risked touching her hair. Fascinated by the mix of colors, he lifted a single strand from her pillow. Winding it around his finger revealed more silver and golden shades of blond than he knew existed.

Her hair was much like the woman she was. A mix of many things, and all of them intriguing. Restless in awakening desire, he had to move, to walk, to consider other things. Slipping from her bed, he dressed and quietly went to explore the house and the garden that, in the passage of weeks, bore the unintrusive but unmistakable stamp of her presence.

An hour and a couple of phone calls later, he strolled the courtyard garden, restored years before by Lincoln. Along with the house at Seventeen Jessamine. Haley had made only a few changes, keeping the garden virtually as it was. Remembering books on gardening lying beside tomes on historic buildings, Jackson didn't doubt it was she who tended the plants and the fountain and the paths, not a hired gardener.

"When?" he asked out loud. "Is gardening solace, Duchess? Time stolen from a busy schedule to think?" If it was, he wondered, regretfully, how many times he'd driven her to her knees tearing trespassing weeds from neatly arranged beds. Finding himself at the curving iron stair that led to the balcony outside her bedroom, Jackson stood, staring up at it. Perhaps he was the trespasser she should have plucked from her life.

"Should have. But didn't." Understanding only a little why she had not, he began to climb the stairs that would lead to Haley. By the time he stepped from the winding stairs to the balcony, he knew the answer to the true riddle of it lay in a whispered confession of the kindling of infatuation at fifteen.

"Fifteen." Scouring his memory, he searched for a girl who could have been Haley at that age. His efforts drew a blank. Finding that she still slept soundly, he crossed to the chair by her bed. He would sit, he would wait. He would plumb his memory again. When she woke, there was much they should resolve.

His gaze settled on his sleeping lover. Thoughts of the girl intrigued him. But not nearly as much as the woman and his response to her. He loved women but had never been in love. He kept his distance from brittle professionals but had never been hostile to a woman. Until Haley.

Staring down at his clenched hands, he remembered that she hadn't intruded in his life. She hadn't battered down the walls he'd erected around himself and his heart. In answering his call for help, she'd simply walked through them as easily as she walked through the door of the barn. From that moment, though he tried to resurrect it, the credo of most of his life didn't apply to her. "But for how long?"

"You're wondering how long this will last."

Looking up, he saw Haley propped on one elbow, watching him. All thoughts except for how well the morning after love became her, fled. "Good morning, sleepyhead." He was not surprised his voice and body were taut with need. Wondering if it could always be this way, he dared let his eyes feast on the loveliness barely covered by a sheet. "Did you sleep well?"

"Better than in a long while." Her cheeks were flushed by the abrasion of a half-day's beard, her eyes were uncommonly bright, uncommonly stunning. "Longer than I can remember."

God help him, he wanted her again. In the space of a heartbeat, he could kick away the chair, tear off his clothing, and join her in her bed. Instead, sanity demanded they talk, that they understand the night and what came next.

"How do I rationalize this, Duchess?" Abruptly leaving his chair, in quick strides he crossed to the door. Standing with his back to her, he looked blindly at the garden. "How do I explain the abandonment of one of the strongest principles in my life? I'm stubborn, opinionated, unreasonable. No one knows better than I that Jackson Cade is the original immovable object. Except..."

"Except when it comes to me." Haley stood at his shoulder, the sheet clasped at her breasts, her feet still bare. Sleepy-eyed and rumpled, she waited for his answer.

"You were the sort of woman I'd loathed for twenty years. Yet one look and I knew you were trouble."

"The evening you called me to River Trace."

"Long before, on your first day at the clinic. I dropped by to speak to Lincoln. One glimpse of you standing in his office, and I turned tail and nearly ran from the building." A bitter smile tilted one corner of his mouth. "A grown man running from a woman barely half his size—sounds ridiculous, doesn't it? But I kept running, avoiding you at all times, at all costs.

"But when our paths crossed, no matter how crowded or busy the place or time, I knew where you were, what you were doing, and with whom. I told myself I didn't like you and never could. And I tried to believe every word."

"Then Lincoln went away, and I was Dancer's last hope."

He turned to her, seeing again the proof of how far he'd strayed from that youthful dedication. "That night, my foundation of lies crumbled beneath my feet."

"Tell me about her." In the only comforting gesture she dared, Haley brushed her fingers through his hair, then let them drift away. Twenty years ago, he would have been fourteen. She could think of but one woman who could hurt him so cruelly at such a tender age. So cruelly a callow girl could sense the hidden pain in her seventeen-year-old Galahad. "Tell me about your mother."

"My mother! Who told you?" His eyes blazed. "Who knows?"

"No one told me. But I can jump to conclusions. Sometimes even logical conclusions." He didn't smile at her whimsy. One didn't smile over a hurt that still lived after two decades.

"No one knew I went looking for her. No one knew I found

her. She was elegant and aloof, a successful businesswoman. No one suspected she had a Southern bumpkin for a son. She intended to keep it that way. Her parting shot as she threw me out of her ritzy office was that she didn't want to see or hear from me again. She'd only married Gus for money. I was deliberately conceived to strengthen her claim on what she thought was millions. When she found his wealth was only in land he would never sell, she deserted the marriage and the child she never wanted.

"She laughed as she said that, but added that there might be some hope for me. After all, I was her son. The thought of that was disgusting."

"So you came home hating her, and anyone remotely like her." Haley could understand that, given his youthfulness. "You never told anyone?"

"Until you, no."

"She was a fool, Jackson." A cruel fool who nearly destroyed him, as only a young untried boy could be destroyed. Haley did not need to be told it was then he began gravitating to the less popular, less pretty girls. Girls less like his mother. And out of his heartache had come her good fortune. "You don't remember an evening and a dance when you were seventeen, do you?"

In a small Southern city like Belle Terre, there were always dances, always parties that included dancing. For all his contrariness, Gus Cade saw to it his sons were a respectable part of the social scene. Beginning with Lady Mary's classes in deportment and learning the fine art of being gentlemen. To employ those acquired graces, he saw to it his sons left the fields and barns in time to make a proper presence. Gus never attended. But his sons certainly did, as part of their duties as Cades.

"When I was seventeen, there were dozens of dances."

"I know." Her thoughts returned to that night. "I imagine the lines blur. Names and faces become a vague jumble of memories. But one has to wonder at the timing in three lives."

"Three?" The room was flooded with light of the new day.

Sounds of the city's routine rose beyond the garden walls. But Jackson's thoughts were of a darkened room and a beautiful woman speaking softly. He could only think of then. Only of her.

"You were fourteen when you had a life-altering encounter." *Encounter*. The word was too mild, but Haley wouldn't elaborate on matters he knew better than she. She wouldn't offer platitudes, or point out that his mother's opinion was only a stranger's twisted thoughts and shouldn't count for more. From her own life she'd learned that at fourteen every judgment counted. Every rejection hurt and kept on hurting, keeping cruel wounds from healing.

She could only imagine how much a mother's rejection scarred a boy who cared enough to seek her out. The threat of tears burned her eyes and constricted her throat. Tears for a boy in pain so devastating it colored the rest of his life. But she couldn't dwell on that. Jackson wouldn't want it.

"Ethan was in college, and I was fifteen and totally alone when you danced with me," she said into the expectant silence. Silence magnified by the sounds of a distant world drifting through the open door. Another world that had little to do with them. Little to do with what had happened in this room. Little to do with Haley, as she smiled, remembering what he had forgotten.

"I was the smallest, the scrawniest, the shyest girl hiding in the shadows of the taller, prettier girls. The new kid in town. The transient no one wanted to make a friend. I didn't wanted to come. My great-aunt, with whom I was staying temporarily, insisted. The first part of the night was the horror I expected. Then the whispers began.

"Jackson Cade was coming." The tilt of the smile that still hovered on her lips quirked in mild self-mockery. "I was such a dumbbell I didn't know who or what a Jackson Cade was. But from the excitement of the other girls, I knew whoever, or whatever, he was pretty special.

"Then I saw you in impeccable formal dress, with your hair

blazing like dark fire beneath the ballroom lights. You were so beautiful. And you were coming straight to me.''

"Beautiful!" he scoffed.

"Don't." With her free hand covering his mouth, she stopped the denial. "Think of a frightened young girl with a tall, smiling young man standing before her asking her to dance. How could he not be beautiful to her? How could he not live in her memories as forever young, forever beautiful?''

Catching her hand, Jackson folded it against his chest. The starched shirt recalled a more recent dance they hadn't finished. But despite the flashing vignettes of the past replaying in his mind, he couldn't recall that other evening. "I'm sorry, Duchess, I don't remember."

Bringing her palm to his lips, he kissed her. Over joined hands resting at the base of his throat, he looked into her eyes. "I wish I could. I wish there had been more than one night, one dance." Each word rang with unmistakable truth. "If I'd known you then, maybe I would be different now."

"It doesn't matter that you don't remember. Even I knew I was distinctly forgettable. At fifteen, I looked twelve. Aunt Gretchen called me a late bloomer. I wasn't even a bud." Haley laughed, though once she would have cried. "That you remembered or forgot me isn't the important factor."

"What is, Haley?" Now he held her hand in both of his, his attention riveted. "What about one night was so important?"

"We danced more than your usual one dance per wallflower, Jackson. We danced the whole night. Every number. I suspect because you felt too sorry for me to abandon me."

From the recesses of Jackson's memory, the elusive image of a frail and tiny girl materialized in his mind. A girl whose hair was white-blond, with no hint of darkened gold. He remembered eyes too big for a pixie face, staring up at him as she followed where he led. Her manner was unsure, but she matched her steps with his with surprising grace. She spoke little, not even to say her name. But she listened as if absorbing every word he said.

Yes, she'd been so frightened, he couldn't bring himself to leave her alone and vulnerable on the sidelines. When that time couldn't be avoided, though he didn't remember his exact words, he remembered the essence of what he wanted to help her understand.

It was strange that after twenty years and so many girls, then as many women, one tiny, frightened girl-child stepped from the netherworld of forgotten memories.

He remembered now that there was something appealing about her. An innocence, a sadness. That, more than the tender heart he'd spent a lifetime denying, kept him dancing with her.

"Believe in yourself. Whether it's that you're beautiful or smart. Believe, even when no one else does." That little wasn't exact, the rest was gone. But he remembered walking away hoping she could believe. Surprised by the recollection he searched her face. Beyond the marvelous eyes, he saw nothing of the girl of his memory. "I said that to you, didn't I?"

"Yes." Her hand moved within his. Not in an effort to gain release, but in a caress. "What I've done with my life, the successes and the failures, I've done alone. But the first spark of confidence to make the needed effort came from that evening. That young, kind boy became my talisman. His words were part of every success. Solace in every failure."

"All I needed was a white horse." Because she touched too closely to the heart of the real Jackson Cade, he strove for disparaging humor. "Maybe a sword for the dragons."

Haley would have no part of his self-deprecation. "You needed no horse to be my shining knight. Your words were your sword. The sword you gave to me, to slay my own dragons."

"I couldn't have done all that for you, Haley. Not in one night. Not at that age." Taking a long breath that lifted his chest beneath their hands, he muttered grimly, "Not at any age.

"The kid you remember has grown up. Given my behavior, I fear that, as predicted, he has become his mother's son. At

Eden's party you sent me away, and I vowed I wouldn't intrude again.'' A derisive snarl pulled back his lips. Disgust
darkened his face. "I rant at you one minute. The next I
haven't the strength to stay away. When you're concerned, I
can't keep my word even to myself.

"You've been hurt enough, Haley. I've done my share of
that hurting in the past weeks. I don't want to add to it. I
shouldn't be here, but I am. Last night should never have
happened, but it did. So, where do we go from here?''

"Wow!'' Haley looked up at him solemnly. "That was
quite a speech. Did you practice while I was sleeping?''

A rueful smile eased the grim lines in Jackson's face. "Part
of it, this morning in the garden.''

"Which part?''

"The part about last night, and not keeping my word.''

"The part about not making love to me.'' Haley slipped her
hand from his clasp. The threat of rain had passed them by,
sunlight falling through the door painted her skin golden and
turned her disheveled hair to a bright, wild halo.

"If you were right before, if making love to you was a
mistake…'' His voice stuttered to a halt. His mouth went dry
as he remembered only a haphazardly draped sheet separated
him from the enchantment of her body. "If it was a mistake,''
he began again. "I'm…''

"You're sorry?'' Her question completed his thought.

Another struggling breath shuddered through him. "Yes.''

"I'm not.'' Her one-handed grip on the sheet relaxed. The
edge slipped an inch. "It wasn't a mistake, and I'm not sorry.
If I were, I wouldn't be standing with my back to the world,
hoping.''

"Hoping?'' The sheet slipped again. She was driving him
crazy and she knew it. His fingers curled into fists, nails scor-
ing his palm against the need to reach for her. "Don't say it
if you don't mean it.''

"I mean it.'' Her gaze was steady. "Every word.''

"Tell me. Let me hear you say what you want.''

"All right.'' Her head lifted, her eyes were brilliant, her

expression solemn. "I want you to make love to me. Here, now. Forever." Her hand opened, the sheet began a slow glide to the floor. Softly she asked, "Will you make love to me, Jackson Cade?"

The sheet had barely tumbled to a pool at her feet when, in answer, he swung her into his arms.

Ten

"**T**hree."

Haley looked up from the glass of juice she'd just poured, a puzzled look on her face.

"You said three lives had been affected significantly at similar ages." Jackson explained his outburst. A response to the thought surfacing out of a quiet mind as he enjoyed a very late brunch. A meal for the famished, Haley had made and packed picnic-style in a basket. To go no further than her tranquil garden.

Hours before, she'd spoken earnestly of the effect of events on teen lives. Then the most pleasurable event in his adult life had swept away both curiosity and coherent thought. Even now it was difficult to concentrate when she looked so fetching in a cotton sundress he knew from watching her dress was the only garment she was wearing. "You were speaking of John Rabb, weren't you?"

As he forced himself to think of the boy, his gaze lingered on the curve of her throat as it gave way to the gradual fullness of her breasts and the first of the cleft accentuated more than hidden by the soft knit. Tearing his attention from the body he had discovered was tiny and deceptively fragile in appearance, but sensual in her needs, he spoke what, in a more lucid moment, seemed obvious. "He was your third teen."

"Yes." She set the pitcher down on the small garden table. A mercurial anxiety displaced the quiet contentment that had enveloped her following the predawn interlude that continued through morning to late afternoon. "I was speaking of Johnny."

Johnny. Jericho had said Haley called the boy Johnny. As Jackson watched her, aware of how perfectly the garden setting became her, he was regretful he'd allowed even this small part of the real world intrude on this peaceful aftermath of passion.

But there was no other time. Merrie had stepped in for him at River Trace. But sooner than he wished, he would need to leave. And there was still much he felt they must resolve. One was Haley's interest in the boy, and her visits to Rabb Town.

Jackson barely suppressed a shiver when he thought of this small woman venturing into the squalid province of the Rabbs. He didn't want her going into the imminent danger that hovered over the settlement like a dirty cloud. Even the swamp-strewn journey to the settlement was difficult, fraught with danger of its own. It was a trek best made on horseback, if one had the time. That the massive SUV she drove instead was built for just such terrain and sufficed, did not ease his concern.

Jackson wanted most desperately to halt her visits into a world that was little like her own. Yet, in a rare moment of diplomatic discretion, he realized he hadn't that right.

"What do you know about the Rabbs, Duchess?" Going carefully, when once he would have been blunt, he asked, "How did you come in contact with them? They aren't quite the sort who take care of their animals. One gets hurt or sick, it gets well on its own or dies. I doubt the word 'veterinarian' is even in their vocabulary. If it were, they would see your services as a waste.''

"I know their reputation, that they're cruel and uncaring with people, as well as animals. Johnny isn't like that. Not really,'' Haley insisted desperately. ''He brought a dog to me,'' she explained, defending her point. ''A scraggly creature that obviously had pups, but lost them all. He found her in the swamp. She was starved and suffering from infection. He had no money.''

Pausing, she watched a bright droplet of water glide down the frosted side of the pitcher. It had soaked into the cloth covering the table, darkening it like a tear, before she looked back at Jackson: ''I haven't mastered the art of turning away a hurting creature for lack of funds. I hope I never do.''

"So you treated the dog.'' A rhetorical question to keep her talking. What he understood best was Haley's compassion.

"I didn't hold out much hope that she would live. But Johnny never gave up. He visited her every day, sitting beside her, praising her, telling her how strong and brave she was.'' Haley looked away, her unfocused gaze settling on the dark green shrub that glittered in the afternoon light. But it was the muted light of the clinic she saw, and a boy sitting patiently by a dog that wasn't his, but would be from that time forward. ''I think he, more than my treatment, saved her. He called her Lady.''

Turning her attention back to Jackson, she continued. ''I told him that. Even so, when he came to take her home with him, he offered a drawing for the cost of her care.'' Haley smiled, remembering. ''If I thought it was good enough, or worth enough.''

Jackson recalled another drawing. One Jericho had singled out. Dual scenes in which a mother dog stood guard, forever, over her last pup. The detail was exquisite, the talent stunning. ''And if you had required payment, it was good enough. In fact, it was really quite astonishing, wasn't it?''

"You've seen his work?'' The look in her eyes was more hopeful than startled.

"Jericho showed me quite a bit of John Rabb's work last night. When the boy's mother brought him in to confess he was responsible for what happened to Dancer, she brought in a folder stuffed with what he'd been doing since he was six."

Haley caught a breath and held it, waiting. The garden was suddenly so quiet, it seemed this small part of their world waited with her. Waited for Jackson's decision. "How is he?" she ventured, at last, into the stillness. "What will happen to him?"

"To answer your first question," Jackson said, "he was quiet but surly. He cooperated, but reluctantly. He must be exhausted by the size of the chip he carries on his shoulder."

"He's afraid, Jackson," she interjected. "Of a lot of things. Too many things a young boy shouldn't have to cope with."

"I know," Jackson admitted. "But to answer your second question, what will happen to the boy is undecided. He's a paradox, but a spectacularly gifted one. After living the life of a Rabb, I imagine he doesn't know who and what he is or should be. This talent must be as bewildering as it is gratifying.

"How does a boy born into such a squalid, uncivilized environment explain or justify that he likes to draw? That he has drawn and continues to draw against what had to be impossible opposition and ridicule speaks of strength? And, Jericho and I are willing to gamble, of unique integrity."

"You can say that after what he did to Dancer?"

"He's a kid, Haley. With a brother old enough to be his father. As much as I hate what he did, I can see how he would fold under Snake's pressure. Because we believe this is the case—rather than that the boy is a budding monster—Jericho and I came up with an option he thinks he can get a judge to agree to."

"And this option is?"

In a rare display of tension, Haley worried the folds of her napkin. Reaching across the tiny table, Jackson took her hand in his. Twining his fingers loosely between hers, he countered with a request. "That, along with apologizing for being a boor, is why I risked getting tossed out on my ear to come to you. Before we discuss options, will you tell me how you compare our lives?''

His fingers moved over hers in small caresses, recalling other touches, other caresses. "Explain to me the similarities and the differences in your life, my life, and John's.''

"You think any of that matters?''

"It does to me. I need to understand what you see in the boy, and what you think can be done for him. Jericho, for all his compassion, sees the boy from a sheriff's standpoint. Mine is that of the injured party. Now I'd like the thoughts of a friend.''

Haley's fingers tightened. A gaze like sun over water searched his, what she saw gave her hope for the boy. "You would help him, despite what he's done? Despite that he's a Rabb?''

"A Rabb and forever a Cade's worst enemy?'' Jackson smiled, finding it difficult to see the faded woman, old before her time, as any sort of enemy. Nor could he bring himself to wage war on a boy of fourteen, no matter his last name, or his crime. "If there's hope at all, yes. I would help. Even a Rabb.''

Taking her hand from his, Haley stood. She needed to think, to consider, to choose her words carefully. Neither of which, she was discovering, came easily when Jackson touched her. When he looked at her as if he would like nothing more than to lie with her and make love to her on the soft moss beneath the massive live oak, she could think of nothing else.

Putting aside the torrid thoughts, wondering if it were his desire or her own she imagined, Haley paced the walk. Gradually, her mind clearing, head down, she pondered what she should say. But no magical phrases came to mind. She had only the truth. And that only as she understood it.

When her decision was made, she found that she had returned to Jackson. Standing at his shoulder, when she looked down at him, she found his cool, calm eyes waiting for hers. Cupping his rugged cheek with her palms, she breathed in the scent of him mingled with the earthy scents of the garden. His scent was her scent. His hair and body bore fragrance of both her shampoo, her soaps, and for a moment she relived the shower they had shared. She remembered the delicious feel of water falling like rain over their joined bodies, as he made love to her again.

How many times over the course of hours had he sated himself in her body? And she with him? Haley didn't know. She didn't care. And like a wanton, she felt again the stir of desire as she stroked the hard line of his jaw.

"Crossroads," she murmured as he turned his mouth into the hollow of her hand. A simple gesture that made it easier to speak what she felt. "Life is about crossroads. Some good, some bad. But there is always one that will most affect our lives.

"You were fourteen when some need sent you seeking your mother. When you found her, she was cruel and foolish. You were too young to understand that all women of her sort weren't the same. And the hate began. By the time you were old enough and wise enough to understand, the habit was too ingrained to change.

"Conversely, I was fifteen and not looking for anything but a hiding place. Then, for one night, you wouldn't let me hide. And I discovered it didn't hurt when people looked at me. I even forgot that they did. With one act of kindness, you set me on the road to confidence. It didn't all just fall into place like a miracle. It was slow, often painful. But every step out of the shadows was progress. After a while, I discovered that I didn't want to hide, or need to hide."

"Crossroads," Jackson murmured. "One negative. One positive. Now Johnny Rabb is at his worst crossroad."

"Or his best."

"Yes," Jackson agreed. "He can go the way of his brothers, and throw away an amazing talent. Or we can help him and end a feud that has gone on for too long and done nothing but harm both the Cades and the Rabbs."

"Johnny's father toppled out of a tree and died from the

accidental discharging of his own gun. He was poaching deer on Cade land. Junior is serving time for attempting to kill Adams. Snake coaxed and bullied Johnny into trying to destroy Dancer,'' Haley recited the iniquities she knew, told to her by Daisy during visits to Rabb Town. ''Where does it all end?''

''With Johnny and his mother. Daisy Rabb has seen the ruin of her family. Now she's down to one son. A son worth salvaging.''

''She can't do it alone, Jackson.''

''She won't have to.'' Pulling her to his lap, he folded his arms about her. ''We'll help.''

''We?'' Haley's heart accelerated, a rush of quiet joy flooded through her. He wanted her to be a part of his plan, perhaps an enduring part of his life.

''I think I can speak for my brothers. Especially Jefferson when he sees John's talent. And Jesse, too, when he realizes the boy's passion for horses. If Jericho has problems with the judicial aspects, Adams knows some of the finest legal minds in the country. But the most important factor is you, Duchess. The boy trusts you. If this venture is to be a success, it will hinge on his confidence in you.''

''I'll help any way I can, Jackson. Surely you know that. But you haven't said what this plan is.''

''Given John's age, Jericho is hoping for a suspended sentence for malicious mischief, or a similar charge *if*—'' Jackson stressed the word ''—if I agree to be John's mentor. Which means the boy will come to live and work at River Trace.''

''Live with y-you?'' Haley stuttered in shock. Whatever she might have hoped for, it would never have been this much. ''Jackson, are you sure? The responsibility would be enormous. But, if it worked, it would be wonderful for Johnny. If it didn't...'' Shaking her head, she whispered softly, ''I don't even want to consider the tragedy it could be.

''Have you thought about Snake's reaction to your plan? And poor Daisy? Have you considered the revenge that creature will take against his own mother when he finds out what

she's done?'' Running her fingers through his hair, catching a
fistful, she raised his face to hers. ''You can't do this, Jackson.
No matter how good it is for Johnny, it's too dangerous for
everyone else.

''Too dangerous…'' Her voice broke, fear shone like dark
fire in her eyes. ''Snake would come after you. You know he
would. I've seen him in Rabb Town, and I've heard him spew
out his hatred for all Cades. But especially you.''

''For no more than getting the short end of a brawl or two,
Duchess.'' Jackson regretted her fear, and at the same time
was inordinately pleased that she cared so deeply. ''Not worth
going to jail for. Even to Snake.''

Haley knew he was dismissing the man too lightly. In her
visits to Daisy, when she pleaded a case for Johnny's talent,
she'd seen the older brother swagger. She'd seen him take
unreasonable offense at the slightest threat to what was truly
a nonexistent dignity. If Jackson had ever bested him, and she
didn't doubt he had, it wouldn't be forgotten.

Abandoning that tack, even as she felt she was letting John
down, she spoke of his mother. ''What of Daisy? She's probably already in trouble with Snake for bringing Johnny in to
Jericho. I wonder, can any of us comprehend what her life will
be if Johnny lives with a Cade as the result of her treason?
Snake will see it as treason, Jackson. And he will have his
revenge. On Daisy first.

''One of the reasons I continued to go to Rabb Town even
after the dog was well, was, of course, for Johnny. But another
part of it was Daisy. Snake abuses her.'' A look of remembered horror lay like dark wounds in Haley's eyes. ''She
wouldn't admit it, and she tried to hide it. But I saw her
bruises. Johnny told me once it was worse since his sisters
married and moved away. He has had a bruise or two, as well.
I suspect from trying to protect his mother from his drunken
brother.''

Jackson reached out to put a reassuring hand on Haley's
arm. ''Snake won't hit his mother anymore. If this goes as
planned, she'll be coming to River Trace with John. Even if

she weren't, Snake won't be a problem. He's been watched for some time by a special government agent. Yancey has informed Jericho that within the week, the final piece of the investigation should be in place. Then, Snake Rabb will be looking at a prison term as long, or longer, than his brother's.

"Until then, and until the trial is finished, Daisy will be protected," Jackson promised grimly. "She's done us a kindness, we owe her one in return."

Haley knew this was about more than returning a kindness. She knew it was Jackson making a difference in the life of a special young boy. As she leaned to kiss him there in the peaceful garden, she whispered. "Crossroads."

Deciding Jesse and Merrie and the crew could manage for a while longer, rising with her from his seat, Jackson laughed softly and agreed, "Our crossroad—the best of all."

"How have you been?" Eden left her daughter, Noelle, to play with Cade, Mr. and Mrs. Brownie, their pups, and Lady. But only under the watchful eye of Adams. As she'd strolled with Haley to the pasture fence, she sensed a new contentment in her companion. "Jackson's arrangement seems to be working."

"It is. It has been, for the most part." Haley turned her back to the pasture. Leaning against a fence post, she watched the crowd gathered in the yard of the manor. "Once Jericho and the lawyer Adams brought in persuaded the judge that Johnny would profit more from what Jackson offered than in detention, it has gone well. At least for the most part."

"The other part being…?" Eden let the question hang, knowing Haley would understand what she was asking.

"The first week was rocky. Johnny was surly. Because of Snake, Daisy was frightened." Haley plucked a dandelion gone to seed. A breath sent seedlings floating like dust motes. Beyond the small shower, she saw Jackson standing with his hand on Johnny's shoulder. "Through it all, Jackson was a paragon of patience."

Following Haley's gaze, Eden murmured, "Amazing, isn't

it? This side of the Cades.'' A gesture included the lot of them, even Gus. ''The softer side none believes in.''

''Adams seems to understand very well. I've never seen a gentler man, or a man more content with his life.''

''Ah, but it wasn't always that way. It began with their father. Gus was a driven and desperate man. He had four wives, lost four wives, and gained four sons. That he loves them is obvious now, but he had no idea how to express it when it mattered most. In hurt and anger, Gus buried his love too deeply for it to show. That left no one to teach the wonderful men you see before you to trust in and believe in their own gentleness.''

''Even Adams?'' Haley's surprise was in her tone.

''Especially Adams,'' Eden answered. ''Like many children who feel unloved, love was what he needed and wanted most. His father's love. It took tragedy, sacrifice and the passage of years before Gus understood the harm he'd done. By then, Adams was convinced *he* was too harsh, too hard. A man who could never love or be loved.''

''Until you proved him wrong,'' Haley ventured.

''Until loving me proved him wrong,'' Eden corrected. ''To a lesser degree, it was the same with Lincoln. It will be with Jackson. Once I thought they would have been different if any one of Gus's wives had been around. But now I'm sure that each would have been the same, eventually, no matter what. You aren't seeing the softer side as much as the truth of Jackson Cade.

''Long ago, each of Gus Cade's sons learned to hide his emotions. In doing so, each was shielding a tender heart. Through loving and being loved, Adams and Lincoln have learned a tender heart isn't a character flaw. In the end they've come to see it as a strength rather than a weakness.''

Her laughter a low, husky tone, Eden added, ''Though he's more than halfway there already, it still might take a while longer for the family firebrand to come to that realization.'' Touching Haley's arm, she added, ''But every minute and every difficulty will be worth their cost in the end.''

"I know," Haley agreed. But she was grateful for the perspective of another woman who loved a Cade.

"Then you're in for the long haul?"

"Yes." Watching the firebrand, the hothead, the brawler, stoop to pick up a baby girl in one arm and a puppy in the other, she murmured, "He hasn't said he loves me yet. But he does."

Eden chuckled. "He's the only one who doesn't know."

"Oh, he knows. But at the moment, he's just not sure of that softer side you described."

"Will it last? Will it pass? Will he hurt you?" Eden knew the litany. She'd been there. So had Linsey. "Jackson doesn't realize quite yet that worrying so profoundly about hurting you is proof those very doubts are unfounded."

"He hasn't stopped to think that each of us brings extra baggage to any new relationship. Or that when something's right, anything that went before doesn't matter. He can't understand that for all his fire, he's the most gentle person I've ever known. The best person I've ever known," Haley murmured.

Eden brushed an unruly lock from Haley's shoulder and tucked it behind her ear. "In other words, you love him."

"In the worst way. And the best."

"When do you plan to tell him?"

Haley didn't answer. For a long moment she stared across the yard, a yard filled with Cades who had come to celebrate Johnny Rabb's birthday. What unique men they were to open their lives and their hearts to the youngest of a family that had been the greatest source of their troubles. Men who had no real understanding of how kind they were.

Turning to the pasture and with her hands braced on the wooden fence rail, remembering a mother who hadn't loved him, she shook her head. "I'm not going to tell him, Eden. Jackson has to believe deep in his heart and irrevocably that I love him. And when he does believe...*if* he does, he will tell me."

"You want him to tell you that you love him. Not that he

loves you." Eden's brows drew down. A thoughtful look filled her eyes as she considered Jackson, and what Haley had said. After a moment, a smile tilted the corners of her mouth. "Perfect. You know your firebrand very well, don't you?"

"I love him, Eden. I have for a long time."

"And one day soon, Jackson will tell you that you do." Eden smiled again. Then she chuckled. Finally, as she linked her arm through Haley's to lead her new friend back to the family, she laughed out loud. "Perfect."

A hectic week later Haley returned to River Trace. This clinic day was blessedly short, but in late autumn twilight came early to the lowcountry. In soft light, the presage of day's end, she approached the veranda where Daisy Rabb sat rocking. Normally the woman would call a greeting. Today, she rocked in silence.

When she reached the base of the stairs, Haley realized Daisy was crying. Not in great, gasping sobs, but with anguished tears sliding unchecked down her cheeks.

"Daisy?" Haley knelt by the rocker, her hand stilling its steady movement. "What's wrong? Are you injured? Is Johnny?"

Daisy didn't speak, her tears didn't stop. As if it were another expression of anguish, she began to rock again. Haley felt sick. This strong woman had lived through bad times and endured worse. She'd lost her tears long ago. "Daisy, is it Johnny?"

"No injury." Daisy Rabb managed to choke out at last. "And not Johnny."

Haley spun about, searching the grounds. "Jackson!"

A rough hand caught Haley's, keeping her from flying down the steps to the barn. "No one is hurt." Daisy's voice was rusty with grief. "There's trouble with one of the horses. Johnny thinks he's been accused. He's in the barn now with Jesse and Jackson, trying to make them believe he didn't hurt the horse."

Daisy's voice broke. For the space of a rasping breath she

said nothing. Then, almost too softly to be heard, she whispered, "The judge will send him to prison. In the end, he'll be no better than his brothers. A wasted life. A wasted talent. A wasted boy."

After patting the gnarled hand that clung to hers, Haley pulled free. "Maybe I can help." Turning, she hurried down the steps and sprinted across the lawn that led to the barn.

Pausing in the doorway, giving her eyes a moment to adjust, she heard the restless stamp of horses's hooves and then Jackson's angry voice calling, "Ho, boy. Ho!" Then, "Haley, no!"

Her own anger flared. Jackson asked her to come. She had. He wouldn't drive her away in time of trouble. She would not be controlled by a stubborn man who suddenly didn't know his own mind. Still blinded by the move from light to darkness, she took another step inside the door. Too late, she realized the nervous shift of hooves was a horse fighting, breaking loose to run.

The massive creature hit her only a glancing blow, but enough to send her reeling against the open door. Pain lanced through her face a second after she saw that Johnny rode the horse. Wondering where on earth the boy was going in such a hurry, and why Jackson was running, she felt her knees give way.

In a dreamlike moment, Haley knew Jackson's strong arms were supporting her. But she didn't know there was a desperation in him. She didn't hear his cry, or the stunned silence of fear, followed by bedlam as he barked orders.

"Jesse, call Cooper. I don't care where he is, or what he's doing, tell him to get here. *Now*." Turning his back on Jesse, as certain that the man would do as he demanded as he was that he would die if anything happened to Haley, Jackson took her to the small room where the guard usually slept.

Haley stirred, breathing in the scents of horses and barns—the identifying scent that would always be the same whether in a tumbledown shack or state-of-the-art barn such as Jackson's.

But on that breath there was a new scent—*his* scent. Jackson's scent. This time totally his and none of hers. A mingling of all he was, of his habits, of his preferences. From it, she remembered he was a man who worked hard and long, bathed often, then returned to work again. That knowledge was there in the aroma of soap and shampoo, in a splash of soothing aftershave born on the heat of his body.

A scent mixed now with the lingering crispness of the autumn air. Suddenly she remembered the racing horse. "Johnny!"

As she struggled to rise, a hand at her shoulder stopped her. "No, Duchess. Lie still. Cooper's on his way."

Keeping her with gentle force, unreasonably fearful of more injuries than were likely or even possible, Jackson sat on the side of the bunk. Eyes as heated as his body stared down at her. Seeing her dishevelment, the fallen coil of her hair lying in a tangle over her shoulder, the red slash across her cheek that tomorrow would begin to discolor, becoming a bruise. "I'm sorry, Duchess. So sorry. I tried to stop Johnny."

Haley's mouth was parched. Her throat was aching and taut. Somewhere a horse whickered softly and stamped, then was soothed by Jesse Lee's singsong voice. The voice cowboys had used on the trail to quiet restless herds of cattle for centuries. It worked as well now with Jackson's finely bred horses.

The sound, then the silence, reminded her of the moment before. She saw the same reminder in the tension of Jackson's lean body. She felt it in his hands as they lay against her shoulders, tightening over the small bones. As if he would comfort her but didn't know how, or if she would accept his comfort.

She knew then that something terrible was wrong. "Jackson? What is it? Has Johnny done something?"

"Shh, be still, sweetheart," he answered in a voice as soothing as Jesse's had been. "Cooper shouldn't be long now."

Touching her face, Haley felt the welt across her cheek. But experience with injuries told her that from the feel of this one nothing was seriously wrong. At best, she would have a headache. At worst, she would have a headache and a shiner. "I'm fine, Jackson. Call Cooper and tell him not to come. All he can do for this is suggest an ice pack. Which you or I can do as well."

Jackson resisted. "He should check you."

"No, Jackson, he should not." Defying the pressure of his hands, she raised herself from the bunk and swung her feet to the floor. She was dizzy and her face ached, but she'd had worse injuries. "This sort of thing happens. Obviously more than you know. Consequently, I've learned to have a pretty good sense of how serious injuries are. On a scale of one to ten, this doesn't even register."

When he looked doubtful, she took his hand in hers. "Darling, you can't hover and constantly stand guard without smothering me. So you just have to learn to trust my judgment."

He was silent as he looked down at their joined hands. Taking a long, unsteady breath, with his fingers tightening over hers, he nodded. "If you're sure."

"I'm sure, Jackson. Have Jesse cancel Cooper's visit."

She watched as he left the small room. At first she was tempted to rise, to follow. A wave of vertigo warned that she should give it a while longer. Then Jackson was back, sitting on the bunk at her side. His face was as bleak as she'd ever seen it.

"Daisy said there was trouble with Johnny." Haley's heart ached. Daisy was right. If the boy violated the court's agreement, he would lose the opportunity that could change his life.

"Not Johnny," Jackson assured her. "We questioned him, but no more than we did the other hands. We wanted to know if he'd seen anyone suspicious around. He panicked and ran away. Now that we know you're okay, Jesse is going after him."

"You haven't said what's wrong."

"A horse was slaughtered in a corral." His fingers tightened over hers. "It was Sugar. Someone cut her throat."

"No." Haley's voice quavered. She'd fallen in love with the little mare the day she rode it. "Johnny wouldn't. He couldn't."

"I know, sweetheart. It seems we have another vandal."

"Snake Rabb?" She muttered. "With guards on duty?"

"He was in custody, on another charge. Jericho's men had been called off. A logical decision with Snake out of action."

"Then who could have done it? Why?" Catching a shuddering breath, with tears in her eyes, she asked, "Why Sugar?"

He turned a sorrowful look at her. "I wish I knew."

Eleven

It was Lady who heard them first.

The little mongrel, who seemed too happy with her new life to cause any fuss, simply wagged her tail, whimpered and danced in place. As the slow, steady clop of horses's hooves grew closer, she did a tail-chasing pirouette and her whole body shivered.

Out of the darkness, with the light from the veranda catching first on the gleaming coats of the horses, then the dark clothing of the riders, the long awaited pair materialized. Daisy was first to make a sound as, in a low breath of relief, she said only his name. "Johnny."

As if that were the signal they waited for, with Daisy between them, Haley and Jackson, hurried from the veranda to the yard. Jesse was none the worse for the hours and the ride through darkness. Johnny's body slumped, his head was down, the brim of his new Stetson shielding his face. He looked tired and defeated, in need of all his energy to stay in the saddle.

It was Jackson who stepped forward, lifting the boy from

the horse. When his boots touched ground, he swayed. Jackson's hand at his shoulder steadied him.

"Mr. Cade." Johnny looked up, stopped. Then swallowed hard, his mouth parched. "Mr. Jesse explained that you were only asking what I might have seen, not accusing me of…of hurting another horse. Considering how I've been acting, so hateful and all, after this I deserve to be sent to jail. I mean, I wouldn't suppose you'd want a mean, ungrateful kid around anymore." The boy swallowed again, harder. "After what I did to Dr. Garrett, I guess you'll be asking Ma and me to leave now."

Regret shimmered in his eyes as he looked at Jackson and finally at Haley. As their gazes collided and held, the apology he didn't know how to speak was there in his earnest face. In that moment, in spite of what had gone before, Haley was proud of him. Johnny Cade was a rare child for more than his artistic talent. A boy who'd survived the harshness of his life without growing bitter or hardened. Haley's smile and nod was her unspoken forgiveness in response to an unspoken apology.

Jackson watched the silent exchange. In it he saw yet another hope for the boy. "Ask you to leave?" he said quietly. "No, Johnny, when you go, it will be because it's what you want."

"You mean it?" Fatigue melted away from the wiry, far too slender body of the youngest Rabb.

"We're just glad you're back. Especially your mom and Lady." A slight push and a grin sent the boy into his mother's arms. "Daisy, I would bet you have a piece of pie left from supper with Johnny's name on it. Even some ice cream, maybe?"

"I do." Daisy smiled over her son's head. "Indeed, I do."

Mother and son were at the veranda steps when Johnny paused and turned back. "Mr. Cade." Jackson only waited, and the boy continued, "I know I said I wouldn't paint with Mr. Jefferson, but if he's still willing, I'd like to give it a try."

"I'll speak with Jefferson again," Jackson promised. "For

now, go along with your mother. Since tomorrow's not a school day, why don't you sleep late in the morning?''

"No, sir." Johnny resisted respectfully. "I'd like to help Mr. Jesse with the horses. If that's okay, I mean."

It was Jesse who spoke up then. "I'd like that. A good hand with a horse ain't something to turn down."

Johnny's face lit up, his pleasure at the compliment visible in the low lights of the veranda. Daisy's arm was around him as she said tearfully, "Thank you, all of you."

Jesse and Jackson were quiet as mother and son disappeared into the house with the faithful little dog at his heels. For the most part, Haley had stood aside, watching, her heart in her throat and tears gathering in her eyes. "He's made the choice he didn't know he had. Johnny Cade is beyond Snake's influence now." She looked from the closing door to the two men beside her. "Thanks to the two of you."

"And you, missy," Jesse interjected. "Seeing you here proved to young John that you cared, too. He's missed you. Tonight he admitted he thought you were staying away because of him."

"We've had a busier week than usual at the clinic during the day, with Lincoln making barn calls in one direction and I in another each evening and morning. I didn't think…" Haley took a thoughtful breath. "I didn't realize he would miss me."

"He's a little in love with you, Haley." Jackson's arm circling her waist pulled her to his side. "As all the Cades are."

Haley said nothing, giving no outward indication that she considered his words more than a casual compliment. Jesse chimed in, calling attention away from her silence. "The Cades and this particular Lee," the cowhand drawled. "Along with half the male population of Belle Terre."

"Jesse," Jackson bristled. "Don't you have something to do? Like unsaddle and bed down these horses?"

"Humph," Jesse snorted, and slipped into his cowboy vernacular. "'Course I got things to do. I don't need no reminder to know when I'm in the way."

"Jesse." When Jesse paused and turned, the reins of the horses he was leading in hand and no real anger on his weathered face, Jackson said, "Thanks for what you did tonight. You claim all you did was explain. But I know better. You've done a lot of talking tonight. Good talking. In the bargain, I suspect you saved a talented boy with a lot to offer the world."

"If I did—" Jesse's smile threatened at last "—I had help." With a touch at the brim of his Stetson, he left them alone.

Jackson and Haley watched him go. He'd stepped through the door and disappeared before Jackson turned to her at last. As she tilted her face to him, he touched the curve of her cheek, gently skirting the darkening bruise. An anathema, the mark of his failure to keep her safe, marring her flawless skin. "You're frowning. Does your face hurt, Duchess? Should I call Cooper?"

"I'm not hurt, and don't call Cooper again." Catching his wrist, she turned her mouth into his palm, letting her lips move over ridged calluses. "The poor man must feel like a yo-yo with all your calls."

Jackson would not be distracted by sympathy for Cooper. "If you're not hurting, why were you frowning?"

"I was thinking about Johnny," she admitted. "Wondering how a boy with his capacity for caring and his compassion could possibly do what he did to Dancer. That cruelty is at odds with what I see in him. I have to believe it's foreign to his nature, no matter his family or the squalor of his life. After seeing him with Lady, an act that destructive boggles the mind. I can't understand how his brother could influence him so completely."

"Think for a minute as Snake would. Suspend your conscience, your decency. Sink to the most unscrupulous level you can to achieve what you want. What would you do?" Haley's frown only deepened. When she turned her head slowly from side to side, Jackson asked, "What threat would be his best leverage?"

"His mother," Haley whispered in a shocked voice.

"Daisy, not Johnny, told Jericho the boy had done as Snake demanded to keep her from harm." Jackson's gaze held Haley's. "Snake Rabb is hardly known for making idle threats."

Haley knew the oldest of Daisy's sons struck his mother. But that he would threaten worse to insure his baby brother would commit an act that was appalling to Johnny, was beyond comprehension. Now that Jackson had voiced the unthinkable, she knew he'd found the answer to the quandary of John Rabb.

But not just of Johnny, of Jackson, as well. For the mutual love between a mother and her son, a love he'd never had, never shared, he offered a helping hand. "Because Johnny wasn't given a choice with Dancer, you're giving him one now. A chance and a choice to live a better life. A decent life."

Stepping into his arms, with her palms she framed his face. "You're a kind and generous man, Jackson Cade."

"For all my warts?" He laughed, as always unable to accept his own goodness.

"*Because of* your warts," Haley emphasized as her palms slipped from his face to his nape, drawing him down to her kiss. "Better still, for all that you are."

Her kiss was sweet, speaking of longing, of endless days spent apart. Of need so deep, he swept her into his arms, taking her to a small gazebo by the river, where ladies of the manor once whiled away humid and hot summer days of the lowcountry.

"Duchess." Her face, as he touched it, was only a pale blur in the cloistering darkness of the small and ancient structure. "I don't want to hurt you."

"You won't." Her fingers were poised at the buttons of her shirt. "Not now. Not ever. Unless you don't want me."

He laughed again, his worry quieted but not vanquished. "I want you. Here." He brushed her fingers away, dispatching both buttons and her shirt with gentle diligence. "Now." As she stepped from her boots, he shimmied her jeans and panties down her hips and away. "For always."

With his own clothing cast aside in a seemingly magical sleight of hand, he stood looking down at her, discovering darkness became her. Then he was bringing her down to him as he sat on the prim and proper seat built for prim and proper ladies. Perceiving that at the end of a long week apart, this moment alone in the dark was their only requisite foreplay, he lifted her across his lap. Easing her down, he watched her shadowed features as she accepted him, making him a part of her as she was of him.

When the joining was complete, her bare arms circled his neck, holding him to her. For a moment neither moved. Savoring the singular wonder of body against body and two becoming one, neither seemed to think or breathe. And somewhere in the utter stillness a night bird sang. A serenade for lovers.

Jackson moved, the thatch at his chest scratching harmlessly against the tips of her breasts. As her back arched in offering, with lips and tongue he soothed away the nonexistent hurt. Haley gasped, then fell quiet. Slowly her hips began to move in concert with his suckling. Both were too much and not enough. His head lifted from her breast, his hands skimmed over her ribs to her back, to tangle in her loose hair and cradle her head. Embracing her, he matched rhythm for rhythm, thrust for thrust.

In cooling autumn darkness their bodies grew damp and slick, gleaming in the little light. Sweet tension spiraled higher, coiled tighter, sparking between them in even sweeter agony. Haley's hands rested at his shoulders. She didn't know her short nails curled into his flesh. He didn't feel the small hurt.

Each time was like the first time with Haley. Each time brought new discoveries, stronger needs, and always the desire for more. More of her touch, her kisses, her body. More of her heart. Until all that was Haley was his.

She was a gift of the night. A gift such as he'd never had or expected to have. Until Haley, sex had been only the empty satisfaction of a need. His passion only for passion's sake.

Until Haley, he'd never wanted more, never needed more, or given more. Until Haley, he'd never truly made love.

With her he was gentler than he thought he knew how to be. More patient and impatient at once, yet more caring for her pleasure than his own. And therein lay her gift to him, as her pleasure became his, and all the greater. With each time and each new delight, heart-shattering hurts that set them apart blurred and faded, then vanished.

For the first time in his life Jackson needed a woman, the same woman, again and again. He needed her now. As if she sensed his craving, she murmured his name, only his name. Then they were fire and flame trembling on the edge of an inferno. No matter that they'd loved before, or how they loved, the culmination had never been like this.

The night was still. But for the soft sounds of lovers, quiet. As the moon slipped behind a cloud the little light that shone on the tiny gazebo was lost. Darkness was complete as they cried together in the shuddering joy of love.

Then into the stillness, into the darkness, into the quiet, Haley whispered love's name. "Jackson."

Jackson straightened from his task of mending saddles. From his vantage point he watched Haley as she worked with Johnny putting a horse through its paces. The sun was bright, kindling lights of gold and silver fire in the wealth of her hair. She came to River Trace as often as she could now. Which for both Jackson and Johnny was never enough. On weekends, at times she stayed the night. And each day it was harder letting her go.

Jefferson and Merrie watched from the corral fence. When the training session was over, they would be taking Johnny and Cade camping in Jefferson's tree house. Johnny thought they were teasing him about the house. He was in for a surprise and a treat when he saw the tree house was a tree house in the truest sense. The result of years of Jefferson's hard work.

And when they were gone? Jackson smiled just thinking

about his plans for the afternoon with Haley. Thanks to Jesse, he could steal the time. With more thanks to Jefferson and Adams and Lincoln for stepping in alternately to free Jesse from his duties at Belle Reve.

Johnny was happy and thriving. Daisy was happy as she proved to be a good housekeeper and an even better cook. Jackson had told her he didn't expect her to work for him, that she owed him nothing. The mother of men who were once his greatest enemies insisted. The breeding and the values that were hers before she made the mistake of marrying a Rabb came shining through.

Everybody was content. Or would be if it weren't for the little things that kept going wrong on the farm. No other horses had been hurt or killed, and nothing major had misfired. But there were small, niggling things—too many, it seemed, to be normal. Broken harnesses. A hay fire, discovered quickly, doused even more quickly. Little things, too numerous to count, too small to merit guards. Such as the saddle he was repairing.

"River Trace," he muttered. "And a barn infested with poltergeists." The seeming happenstances worried him, but as long as no more horses were lost, not enough to spoil the afternoon with Haley. An afternoon he hoped would be the most memorable in both their lives.

A half hour later, Johnny, Jefferson, and Merrie had gone to pick up Cade. Haley was watching him finish the saddle when Daisy called from the house. "Telephone message for you, Miss Haley. A man called saying he had news of your brother, Ethan. He will meet you in an hour at the house on Jessamine Street."

"News of Ethan." Haley leaped from her seat by Jackson.

"The caller, he didn't give his name?" Jackson frowned.

"No, sir." Daisy replied. "He said his name didn't matter, Miss Haley would know who was calling."

"Yancey." Haley turned back to Jackson. "He's the only one it could have been. I have to go."

Jackson caught her hand as she turned. "I'll go with you."

"No." Gradually, she extracted her fingers from his clasp. What Yancey had to tell her would be confidential. Though both she and Yancey trusted Jackson, for his own sake he shouldn't be privy to some of the information she might be given. "I'll call you, I promise. If not tonight, then early tomorrow."

Rising on tiptoe, she kissed him. Before he could think of a reason to stop her, she was gone. Too soon her truck was blocked from view by the row of oaks. Without Haley, the afternoon he'd anticipated held the specter of loneliness.

"A hundred people could be here. A thousand. If Haley isn't one of them, River Trace is lonely. I'm lonely." For another moment he stared at the empty road with dust beginning to settle again. Then he turned away.

Jackson picked up his fork, then laid it down again. As he had twice before. He couldn't eat and watch the clock. But that didn't matter. He had no appetite, not even for Daisy's best country-style steak. Sliding back his chair abruptly, he stalked to the telephone. He didn't know how many times he'd dialed Haley's number, but he dialed it once again. As he willed that she answer, the telephone rang incessantly in his ear. "She promised she would call last night or this afternoon. It's nearly dark, she isn't home."

"Could be she's on her way here," Daisy suggested.

"She would call first. Especially since it's so late." Jackson lifted the receiver again. This time the telephone was answered. "Lincoln. I'm trying to reach Haley. Do you know where she might be? She called in sick? Last night?" With his fingertips he pressed against the ache at his temples. "She was fine last night. Yancey called—he was to meet her at Jessamine Street with news of her brother."

Jackson listened awhile longer. When he hung up, he was pale. "Jericho was having dinner at Lincoln's. He said Yancey was called to investigate a bombing incident in Seattle two days ago.

"I have to go. I have to see for myself that she isn't too ill to answer the phone." He rushed from the room.

Daisy didn't move or speak until she heard his car driving away. In an uneasy tone, remembering a slaughtered horse, to no one she whispered, "Whatever is wrong, I hope it isn't part of the mischief that's happening here."

"If she didn't work today, and she isn't home, then where is she?" Jackson paced the garden at Seventeen Jessamine like a tiger trapped in a cage. For the tenth time he growled, "Who the hell called about her brother if it wasn't Yancey?"

"I spoke to Yancey," Jericho said. "He didn't call."

Adams and Lincoln and Jefferson stood in a cluster by the live oak, but neither could offer any more than Jericho. No one had seen Haley. No one had heard from her. No one knew where she was.

"This isn't like her." Lincoln was adamant. He'd known her too many years to not have learned she was responsible to the letter, prompt to the minute. "I don't want to be the harbinger of bad news, but if she said she would call, she would have. If she was ill, she would have said she was."

"Is there any trace of her truck?" Adams directed his question at Jericho. When the sheriff only shook his head, he turned to Jefferson. "Is it possible she decided to come to the tree house and got lost?"

"There's one way in, and the same way out." Jefferson grimaced, wishing that had been the case. "She couldn't get lost. If she got stuck, Merrie and the boys and I would have seen her truck on the trail on our way home."

"Then where is she?" Jackson was barely clinging to his control. He wanted to run down the peaceful street, knocking on doors, demanding that someone tell him they'd seen her. He studied her house. Every inch had been thoroughly checked. No one was that familiar with her clothing, but nothing appeared to be missing. If any luggage was missing, then she had a lot. "She wouldn't just pick up and leave. She had too much invested in her life in Belle Terre. Too much invested in us.''

"I'm going to initiate a background check first thing in the morning. To see if there's someone or something in her past that might offer a clue. Who knows—'' Jericho shrugged a massive shoulder ''—she might be off on an involved and serious barn call.''

It was Lincoln's turn to shake his head. "She wouldn't do that. I can't think of any situation in which she couldn't spare a minute. But if, by some chance, she couldn't call, Haley would ask someone else to do it for her.

"As far as background goes, I knew her pretty well in school—beyond her family, there was no one special in her life. I can't speak about later. After vet school, we kept in touch, but not on a close, personal level.''

"Haley was married.'' Jackson stood dejected, his hands in his pockets. "It was an abusive relationship and over quickly. She took back her maiden name. The man, Todd...'' A bleak look met Jericho's. "I can't recall his last name.''

"Does Haley know where he is now?'' Jericho was instantly alert, his Native American heritage evident in his rugged face.

"Prison.'' Jackson felt a cold quiver down his spine. "He's in prison. Haley was to be notified when he was released. My God, Jericho. Among other things, he was sadistic, and a stalker.''

"Then maybe I won't wait until tomorrow to start the check. The sooner we know where this Todd person is, the better we'll know where to start.'' Jericho plucked his wide-brimmed hat from the garden table. "I'm heading downtown now to begin. Where will you be, Jackson, if I should need you?''

"Here.'' He didn't hesitate. "I'll be here, Jericho.''

"This is it.'' Jericho laid the computer report before Jackson. It was midday of the second day. An eternity that crept by slowly. "Todd Flynn, alias Jones, alias Dean, was released for good behavior three weeks ago. Haley said there was a notation on file indicating she was to be alerted of his release by telephone or mail. But it's not here.''

Jackson took the page, scanned the impersonal lines, then tossed it on Jericho's desk. "Why not?"

"What's going on?" Yancey Hamilton stood in the doorway. He was lean, mean, tall, dark, and handsome, and clearly exhausted. "To answer your question before you ask, since my name was used in vain, I hurried the investigation along to the point I could turn it over to a subordinate and hopped on the first plane out of Seattle.''

"The caller didn't use your name." Jackson was as weary as Yancey looked. "Haley assumed it was you, since it concerned a message about or from her brother.''

"Ethan?" Yancey was instantly tense, every shred of fatigue falling away. "The caller knew about Ethan Garrett?"

Jackson collapsed into a chair, rubbing his burning eyes with his thumbs and forefingers. "He called him by name.''

"Then Simon McKinzie has a serious breach of security, or this is someone privy to family information. If it's the latter, and I hope to God it is," Yancey said fervently, "then it's someone who knew Ethan Garrett had a dangerous job, and that Haley and her parents were always worried about him. He, whoever he is, would know, too, that Ethan sent messages by strange men. Strange to the family, that is," he corrected.

"Flynn," Jackson whispered grimly. "The vicious son of a bitch has her.''

"We don't know that." Jericho came to stand by Jackson. "We have to keep an open mind. Open to all possibilities.''

Jericho didn't want to tell Jackson that he was sending men and women out to check the road from River Trace to Belle Terre, and along with it, the river and the swamps that flanked it. Both teams were comprised of officers specially trained in reading the terrain and the roads by the same master tracker. If Haley's car had skidded off the road into scrub or, God forbid, into the river, his people would find it.

"What can I do?" Yancey asked. He'd known Jericho too

long, and understood his thorough and methodical manner of investigating too well to just jump in. If he could help, the sheriff would know how best to use him.

"You can touch base with Simon." Jericho hadn't worked under the auspices of the clandestine government organization The Black Watch, but he'd worked with Simon and Simon's people. If there was a clue to be found, The Watch would find it. Out of respect for Yancey, and evidently Ethan Garrett, too, if for no other reason. "Explain the situation. Find out what he thinks."

"Will do." With a small salute of respect, Yancey turned to go. Pausing by Jackson, he said, "Go home, get some rest. You can't do her any good if you're exhausted."

"I'm going back to Jessamine Street," Jackson replied. "If I can sleep anywhere, it will be there."

Yancey's mouth quirked. Not in a smile, but in recognition of a long-held belief. "You've got it bad, haven't you? Just like Jesse said."

"Yeah," Jackson admitted. "Maybe if I'd known it as soon as the rest of you knew, this wouldn't have happened. Maybe I could have protected her."

"Protect Haley?" Yancey did laugh then, but not in mirth. "It's a nice thought, buddy, but not something she would want or need. After her marriage and the time that followed, Ethan saw to it that she could protect herself. She may be barely more than five feet nothing, but she can fight like a tiger.

"If this character has her, he also has his hands full."

"You're talking about this." Jericho scaled a page across his desk. Yancey caught it but didn't bother to read it.

"It says the bastard stalked her after the divorce. Then he kidnapped her, holding her hostage for days. He didn't rape her." Yancey seethed with rage. "But only because a freak accident had left him irreparably impotent. So he branded her instead."

Jackson's drooping shoulders came up. His gaze was riveted on Yancey's face. "You know what he did to her?"

"I know." Yancey's expression was bitter. His gaze, diamond-hard. "Ethan and I went after her. If Haley hadn't stopped him, Ethan would have killed the bastard. But she did stop him, for Ethan's own sake, not for Todd's. If the lowlife has her, it's a damn poor way to repay her for his life. Frankly, I think we have another hostage situation."

"Will he hurt her?" Jackson's voice was devoid of emotion. His mind was too chaotic to express a single reaction.

Yancey didn't answer for a heavy moment. On a hoarse sigh, he nodded abruptly. "He's done it before, and I'm scared witless he will again.

"I'm sorry, Jackson. I could lie, but what the hell would that accomplish? If he does, he'd better run far and hide deep, because Ethan Garrett will hunt him down."

"So far, we don't know for certain he has her," Jericho broke in. The focus was narrowing too exclusively to one option, without proof. Wearily, he glanced at his watch. "It's late. There's nothing more we can do tonight. Go home, Yancey. Go home, or to Jessamine Street, Jackson. Rest if you can. My field teams will start again at sunup, if you'd like to join them."

Busy work for the tormented mind. Jackson recognized the ploy. But he was grateful for the opportunity. Nothing would help. Nothing would ease the hurt and worry. But the physical activity would at least speed the solitary hours along.

Solitary. He'd been surrounded by family and friends almost constantly, and without Haley, he felt alone. She'd captured one small place in his unwilling heart from the first. A place that had grown and grown until in was all of him, heart and soul. Would he have a soul without her? Could he live without his heart? Would he want to?

"Jackson." Jericho touched his arm. "Yancey and I will walk you out. Did you drive downtown? Or can I give you a lift?"

Rousing, he stared at Jericho, assimilating what he'd said. "No," he managed to answer after a lengthy wait. "I'll walk. Maybe the night air will clear my head."

As Jericho stepped past, Jackson caught his arm. "If he hurts her, Ethan Garrett won't get a chance at him, Jericho."

The sheriff held his suffering friend's glare for a long time. With a curt tilt of his head, he said, "I know. That's why we're going to find her before he hurts her."

"If it isn't too late already."

"Speed isn't his style." Yancey stood in the doorway again. This time waiting for his friends. "He likes to draw it out. He gets off on fear. Ethan worked as a profiler once. He says nutcases like this one have to hone the fear to a certain level. If he can't, the kicks aren't there.

"The best thing Haley has going for her is that she understands that. She's familiar with his methods and his needs."

"Familiar." Jackson spat the word.

"Yeah." Jericho flung an arm around the smaller man's shoulders. "Familiar as in she can beat him at his own game."

"But can she?"

"Between them, my money's on Haley." With his free hand, Jericho dropped his Stetson onto his dark head.

"Mine, too," Yancey added as he fell into step with them.

"Yancey has personal knowledge of Haley and Flynn. Beyond what's written in the reports, you don't, Jericho."

"Don't need to," the big man insisted. "I know Haley. That's enough. Should be enough for you, Jackson Cade."

"Maybe." The ache in Jackson's heart eased only a little. It was a start. By tomorrow he would shake off the stupor and inertia that had enveloped his body and mind. He would be thinking. With something to contribute toward finding Haley and bringing her home. Home to him. Home to his arms.

"No," he said with conviction. "Not maybe. Exactly."

Twelve

Jefferson paced the shoulder of the rarely traveled road. Each step drawn out, graceful. He could have been a dancer performing a dramatic segment of a ballet. Instead, he was a master tracker, searching for a lost friend.

Dust barely riffled around the soles of his tall boots then settled swiftly in the wake of each step. In the days since the search began, Jefferson had been rock-steady, calmly efficient. He never hurried, never showed any sign of strain, or stress, or fatigue. There was little indication he was even remotely affected by the suddenly unseasonable heat.

He'd simply abandoned his usual broad-brimmed hat, tied a bandanna about his head, and continued his meticulous exploration. Now the scarlet strip angled across his forehead was saturated. Sweat dripped down his face, channeling through clinging dust. Only an occasional forearm swiping across his brow hinted at eyes burning from the salt of his body.

Carefully, Jackson followed a few paces behind. Realizing a man like Jackson was better busy than idle, Jericho had suggested he accompany his trackers. For a while, he did. When, on a hunch, Jefferson split from the main group, so did Jackson.

He was grateful for the men and women and their trained dogs, but his faith lay in his younger brother. Jefferson knew the country. He lived with the earth, not on it. He communed with it, listening as it spoke to him. Jackson prayed it was so today.

Haley had been missing for four days.

Four days. The number and images of Haley tracked through his mind, running roughshod over any other thought he might have. *Where is she? How is she? Has the bastard hurt her?*

He couldn't think of anything else. He couldn't sleep. He couldn't eat. *I can't live without her.*

The last thought brought him up short. Fists clenched, eyes burning, he knew that it was true. He'd become so infatuated with Haley, he'd looked no further than the next hour, the next day, the next week. When she was with him, he lived for the moment.

Now that she'd vanished, he knew he didn't want hours, or days, or weeks with her. *I want forever.*

On a road that was only a meandering track, with the scent of dust in his lungs, Jackson Cade raised his eyes to a cloudless sky. His lips moved silently, shaping one word, "Please."

He didn't know how long he stood there offering up his plea, but when he looked again at the road, Jefferson had moved from sight. Reverting to a little-used name, he called, "Jeffie."

"I'm here, Jackson." The youngest of the Cades was striding back to him. As if it had talons, rather than thorns and spikes, underbrush separating the road from swamp clawed at him. His face grim, Jefferson only brushed each away.

Something had changed. "Jeffie?" Jackson searched his brother's face. "You've found her! You've found Haley."

"No." Jefferson stood in the road, in the dust, beneath the burning sun. "I haven't found her."

"Then what?" Jackson was more afraid than he'd ever been.

Jefferson inhaled a labored breath. "Haley's truck." A small jerk of his hand indicated the road and a looping curve skirting the edge of the swamp, then disappearing into more scrub. "Whoever was driving hit an alligator. The truck rolled over in the swamp."

In panic Jackson lunged forward. Jefferson caught him in a bear hug. "We don't know she was in the truck. We won't know anything until Jericho gets the proper crews out here." When he was sure Jackson was listening, Jefferson released him. "From the condition of the gator, this hasn't just happened."

"How long?"

"A couple of days," Jefferson judged. "Maybe longer."

"No." Jefferson held him tighter.

"That it's her truck doesn't mean she was in it." Dreading what he had to say, Jefferson waited until his brother calmed. "If she was," he muttered regretfully. "She doesn't need you now."

The silence was complete. As brother stared at brother, there were no words either could say.

Silently, Jackson sat apart from the tumult invading the desolate spit called Lost Point. He couldn't see the site or the crane that would be raising Haley's SUV from the brackish water. His brothers waited with him, as silently. Offering neither empty words nor emptier platitudes.

Abruptly the furor quieted. Four Cades sat unmoving as Jericho appeared on the road. They watched as he walked to them.

"He's smiling," Jefferson whispered hoarsely.

When Jericho was close enough to be heard, he stopped. The composed, normally stoic sheriff truly was smiling. "She isn't there. The doors are locked, the windows closed and still intact. There's no room for error. Haley wasn't in the truck when it hit the gator and rolled into the water. Only the driver's there.

"We won't have positive identification or cause of death for a while. But my instincts say it's Todd Flynn, and that Haley isn't with him means she's alive. Somewhere."

Joy burst from three Cades. One stood inarticulately grateful. They faced a terrible puzzle. But there was still hope.

Linsey poured coffee. In heat that bore down like an anvil, the men who filled her kitchen thrived on the strong brew. Pausing to ruffle young Cade's hair as he sat on Lincoln's knee, she listened to their conversation.

The Cades, Jericho, Yancey, Jesse, and Johnny—and even Davis Cooper—were crowded into the small room. Eight grim men and two boys wracking their minds for solutions.

Where was Haley? What had Todd Flynn done with her? What had he been doing on a desolate road that went nowhere? How much longer did Haley have? That was the conundrum. Hashed and rehashed, with no one offering an answer. In the heat, timing was critical.

With Johnny at his side, Cade sat quietly. Though he understood the gravity of the situation, he was happy to be with Lincoln and the men he admired. Worried his young presence was a bother, Linsey went to Lincoln to take the boy away.

"No, Mom," Cade resisted. "I'm not in the way, and I'm not disturbing anything. Please." The last was long and pleading.

"He's okay, sweetheart." Lincoln looked up at her with a painful smile. Mingled with his concern for his brother, she saw gratitude that his own small family was safe. Dropping a kiss on Lincoln's forehead, with a caressing touch for Cade, she returned to the counter to make yet another pot of coffee.

"I can't understand, what this feller was doing way off there?" Jesse voiced again the question asked countless times. When he'd arrived, he admitted he'd worried at River Trace until he couldn't bear to wait any longer. Leaving Jackson's stock in the hands of his crew, he and Johnny had come to help.

"An out-of-the-way place like that—it doesn't make a lot of sense," Yancey put in. "Some of the natives don't know it exists."

"The last place I would have suspected," Jericho admitted. "Thank God, Jefferson did."

"That still doesn't answer the question of why he was there." Lincoln slipped an arm more closely about Cade.

"Maybe he didn't mean to go there, Dad," Cade's young voice piped in as he looked up at his father.

The room went still. All eyes turned to Lincoln's son.

"What do you mean, Cade?" Lincoln stared down at this child he'd already discovered possessed the wisdom of Solomon.

"Maybe he was lost. A place like Lost Point is easy to find when you're lost, too. Like Mom and me were when we found it."

Attention shifted to Linsey. "You went to Lost Point?"

"Not on purpose," she confessed. "I took a wrong turn at the maze of roads called Six Chances. We ended up at Lost Point. I only knew the name because a jokester's sign said since I was there I was likely lost, but I'd found Lost Point."

"When was this?" Jericho asked.

"Over a year ago."

"Where had you been?" Adams addressed Cade.

"Mom took me to the old tenant house ruins to show me the cellar. In case the cover Dad replaced ever slipped. She didn't want me to fall in or get trapped."

"The tenant house." Jackson was afraid to believe what he was thinking. Yet as he said it, he was certain. Rising from his chair, with conviction and hope, he said, "Haley's in the cellar. I know she is. Just as, deep down, I knew she wasn't in her truck in the swamp. I was afraid to trust my instinct then, but no more."

He looked from brothers to friends. "She's there. Tonight,

when I stop by the inn to report to Colonel and Mrs. Garrett, the news will be good. We'll find her at the ruins.''

The way was rough, the terrain uneven. The path the cavalcade of vehicles traveled through the dense forest was not a road but the remembered passage of a tornado. Limbless trees stood in testament of the brutal force of that erratic storm. A deadly whim of nature that wreaked its havoc then was gone, leaving destruction and this broken track in its wake.

At the time Lincoln had brought in a crew to clear away the debris. But in the nearly two years following the storm, the forest had begun to take back its own. Failing light and new growth slowed their passage when every nerve screamed, ''Hurry!''

''How did a stranger find this place?'' Davis Cooper asked in dreadful awe when he caught his first glimpse of the ruin that was no more than a sunken, crumbling foundation.

''Only God can answer that, and any number of questions now,'' Jericho responded as he was sliding from the car to race the last little distance to the cellar.

In minutes, muscles trembling from hurried efforts to remove debris from the heavy cover, Adams, Lincoln, Jefferson, and friends watched Jackson bring a tired, dirty, incredibly beautiful Haley from the dusty earthen pit.

She didn't speak, she didn't cry. With eyes unaccustomed to even a little light, and weak from hunger, she swayed on her feet. Then she smiled. As she burrowed deeper into Jackson's embrace, she understood Ethan's creed that love made him invincible. She'd survived the long, dark hours by loving and being loved by Jackson. She would have willed herself to survive longer. For she believed with all her heart that somehow he would find her.

Because he loved her.

With his tears wet against her cheek, she lifted her lips to his, murmuring softly, hoarsely, ''I knew you would come.''

Music and laughter filled the air. River Trace and all its guests were dressed in their festive best. Friends and family had come together to celebrate an end and a beginning.

No one thought it odd that Daisy Rabb was responsible for both refreshments and flowers. Usurping even Cullen, Eden's Pacific Island wonder and majordomo at the inn. As Johnny with his art and the horses, Daisy had blossomed in her new environment. The only mystery was how she ever married a Rabb.

Flanked by her mother and father and her beloved brother Ethan, after two weeks of recovery Haley was radiant. Her gown for this celebration of her life was simple, a complement for her hair and eyes and skin. The slim column of rich cream fit her like a glove. And, though she was still too slender, it was easy to see the family resemblance as, arm in arm, with her parents she took them through the crowd, introducing them to her new friends, explaining how important each had been in her life. How instrumental in preserving it. Especially Jefferson and Cade.

"The important element in your daughter's survival, Colonel and Mrs. Garrett, was Haley, and the survival skills Ethan taught her." Yancey bent to kiss her bare shoulder, then led her parents away to show them Dancer, the pride of River Trace.

"Yancey's right. This could have ended tragically if it weren't for Haley's spirit and stamina." Jackson added, "Spirit, stamina and what you taught her, Ethan."

With his arm newly casted and still weary from his own recent ordeal, Ethan Garrett laughed. Though he was more than a foot taller, with hair darkened to a rich, golden brown and his face bearing evidence of his rugged life, when he smiled he could pass for Haley's twin. "She was a good pupil. A lady warrior."

"Lady warrior—the name fits." Sliding an arm around her, Jackson pulled Haley back against him. "Would you mind if I steal your sister away for a while?"

Upon his arrival, Ethan Garrett made it a priority to discover all he could about the man his sister loved so completely. He'd learned his first impression was correct. Jackson Cade was a maverick, but a man of honor and a gentleman. A man who stood strong and went down hard. Even in love.

He smiled at the man so much like himself. "Would it matter if I did mind, Jackson Cade?"

"Truthfully? No."

Pleased, Ethan chuckled. "I didn't think so."

"You have my thanks, Ethan, for my lady." Then Jackson was running with her to the privacy of the gazebo.

Sitting with her, he took her hand. After two weeks of recovery, the bruises had begun to fade. Her nails were no longer broken and torn from the battle waged against superior strength when she was taken from Jessamine Street.

Horror dispelled, her eyes were bright, not glazed and sunken from hunger and dehydration. Her hair was clean and shining. She was beautiful now. She was beautiful then, after four days trapped in the sweltering cellar.

Medical records confirmed the driver had been Flynn. An autopsy found he'd sustained a blow to the head in the accident, likely drowning while he was unconscious. An investigation discovered he'd cultivated a friendly relationship with a young secretary while he enjoyed the freedom of a trustee in a minimum-security facility. A trust he capitalized on to gain unsuspected access to records containing Haley's address. It had been as easy to erase any mention of her from his file. Thus, when he was paroled, there was no reference to a required call or letter of notification of his release. And nothing to intercept.

Todd had bragged to Haley that he was behind the vandalism at her lover's barn. He regaled her with the story of how he killed Sugar. Simply because he'd seen her ride the little mare. And simply because he could. He'd found it funny that the Rabbs, who were strangers to him, were suspected of his mischief and atrocity.

Latent fingerprints had tentatively proved he was behind the mischief he'd claimed. But the rest—how he found the ruin, where he was going when he died, and if he intended to leave her in the cellar forever—could only be conjecture.

For Haley, his promise that he would abandon her to die in the ruin was far from conjecture. She'd believed every word.

"Hey." Folding her fingers in his, Jackson brought them to his lips. A kiss like a breath brushed over her knuckles, calling her back to him. "No bad thoughts allowed today."

When she only smiled, he ventured, "You were thinking of him, weren't you?"

Haley nodded. "Of Todd and of you. Of how he underestimated Jackson Cade, and the power of love. Along with the help of your brothers and the best of friends."

"Yeah," Jackson agreed. Settling back against the rail of the gazebo, her hand still in his, he watched the river. The sun was bright, the day warm, and Haley was safe beside him. All was right in his world. This day wasn't about the past. It was a celebration of the first day of the future. His future with Haley and hers with him.

"We shouldn't steal away like this," she said at last, breaking the comfortable silence. There was secret, delightful laughter in her eyes as she turned to him, remembering as he did their last interlude in the gazebo. "You have guests."

"*We* have guests," he corrected. "You know this is more than a party, don't you? And the gown Eden chose isn't simply a gown?"

Haley looked down at the exquisite garment. "Eden made a marvelous choice. It's lovely."

"Not nearly as lovely as you, Duchess." As he called the name that began in derision and became an endearment, he folded both hands over her shoulders. "If you'll have me, I want to spend my life with you. Beginning with a wedding tonight. Everything's in place, all you have to do is say yes. You love me, Duchess. I know you do. Almost as much as I love you."

"All right, Jackson."

"I'm hotheaded, opinionated. My temper can be hellacious, but it's nothing you can't tame. Haven't tamed. I…" His grip was painful. But what was a little ache when it accompanied this awkward, wonderful declaration she'd waited forever to hear?

His fingers flexed at her shoulders. "What did you say?"

"I said yes, Jackson."

"Because you love me." He said the words surely, confidently, as if he believed them with all his heart. As she'd promised Eden someday he would.

Laughing, she went into his arms, murmuring as her lips caressed his. "I thought you would never tell me."

"That I love you?" he puzzled as he kissed her.

"Yes, my stubborn, opinionated, beloved firebrand," she whispered indulgently. "That, too."

* * * * *

And now turn the page
for a sneak preview of

THE REDEMPTION OF JEFFERSON CADE

On sale in January 2002
from Silhouette Desire

One

_____

The splash wasn't loud enough to draw him from sleep, but it did. As naturally as breathing, Jefferson reached for Marissa. He was alone. She had dressed and gone. In her place lay the scarf he'd taken from her hair. Catching up his jeans, he slipped into them and moved to the ladder that would take him to the ground.

"No," Marissa called from the water's edge. Her heart was in her eyes as she looked up at him. "Don't come down, Jefferson. I don't think I could bear to leave if you do."

"Don't go," he said softly, though he knew it was futile.

Marissa didn't answer. As he stopped short of the first rung, she turned to toss a small stone into the pond. Droplets scattered like diamonds. Ripples radiated from the tiny epicenter, glittering waves washed the shore at her feet. The water's surface was as calm as dark glass before she spoke again.

"This day and this place have been magic. So I thought that, for a little while, the pond could be a wishing well. Perhaps it was greedy of me, but I've made two wishes."

He wanted to climb down and take her in his arms. Instead, he asked, "What did you wish, Marissa?"

When she looked up at him, her dark eyes glittered and her smile was bittersweet. "First I wished you wouldn't forget me."

Jefferson said nothing. It was a wish already granted. How could a man forget a woman like none he'd ever known. "And the second?" he asked hoarsely. "What did you wish next?"

"The impossible."

"Maybe it doesn't have to be, sweetheart."

Her smile faltered. "You're wrong, my beloved friend. Though I've wished with all my heart, we won't meet again."

A knife in his heart couldn't hurt as much. "Wishing wells grant three wishes. Will you wish again?"

"Yes." The stone was already in her hand.

"Will you tell me the last?"

"Not this time. Not this wish."

Jefferson didn't pry. And though he knew what would follow the splash of the last stone, he wasn't ready for it.

"Goodbye, Jefferson Cade." Her voice was soft, her words halting. "I won't forget you. I won't forget this day."

"Marissa." He waited until she turned back, until their eyes met. "If ever you need me...I'll come for you."

"I know," she acknowledged quietly, and with a shattered smile she turned away again.

He wanted to call out to her, to ask her again to stay. Instead, as silent as the wilderness, he watched her go.

At the far shore, by the edge for the path, she stopped and raised a hand in farewell. At that moment, the storm for which the land had lain in wait lashed out with a blinding bolt of lightning and an earthquaking rumble of thunder. When the world was quiet again, the path was empty. Marissa was gone from his life.

Heavy rain was now falling, Jefferson paused at the edge of the clearing. Droplets gathered on his clothing, his hair and on the sweep of his lashes. Through the downpour, his gaze sought the half-hidden bower where he'd made love to Marissa Claire Alexandre beneath a canopy of green.

His sketch pad shielded against his body, a keepsake folded against his heart, he stood committing to memory this day, this place. Someday he would paint it, melding sketches and memories on canvas. Someday, but not yet.

Rain fell harder, spattering over the pond like stones in a wishing well. "One wish is true, Marissa."

Lightning flickered, thunder whispered. As quickly as it came, the rain stopped. As a mist shrouded the land, Jefferson waited for one more glimpse that never came. It didn't matter.

"I won't forget."

Then he turned away. The wilderness was his sanctuary. As a boy he'd come in search of solace. As a man he came seeking peace. In all the years, neither the solace nor the peace had been complete, but it served. For boy and man, it served. Until this day. Though the wilderness had been an abiding part of his life, he knew it could never be the same.

He wouldn't come again.

CALL THE ONES YOU LOVE OVER THE HOLIDAYS!

Save $25 off future book purchases when you buy any four Harlequin® or Silhouette® books in October, November and December 2001,

PLUS

receive a phone card good for 15 minutes of long-distance calls to anyone you want in North America!

WHAT AN INCREDIBLE DEAL!

Just fill out this form and attach 4 proofs of purchase (cash register receipts) from October, November and December 2001 books, and Harlequin Books will send you a coupon booklet worth a total savings of $25 off future purchases of Harlequin® and Silhouette® books, AND a 15-minute phone card to call the ones you love, anywhere in North America.

Please send this form, along with your cash register receipts
as proofs of purchase, to:
In the USA: Harlequin Books, P.O. Box 9057, Buffalo, NY 14269-9057
In Canada: Harlequin Books, P.O. Box 622, Fort Erie, Ontario L2A 5X3
Cash register receipts must be dated no later than December 31, 2001.
Limit of 1 coupon booklet and phone card per household.
Please allow 4-6 weeks for delivery.

I accept your offer! Please send me my coupon booklet and a 15-minute phone card:

Name: _____

Address: _____ City: _____

State/Prov.: _____ Zip/Postal Code: _____

Account Number (if available): _____

---

097 KJB DAGL
PHQ4012

If you enjoyed what you just read,
then we've got an offer you can't resist!

Take 2 bestselling love stories FREE!
Plus get a FREE surprise gift!

Clip this page and mail it to Silhouette Reader Service™

IN U.S.A.
3010 Walden Ave.
P.O. Box 1867
Buffalo, N.Y. 14240-1867

IN CANADA
P.O. Box 609
Fort Erie, Ontario
L2A 5X3

YES! Please send me 2 free Silhouette Desire® novels and my free surprise gift. After receiving them, if I don't wish to receive anymore, I can return the shipping statement marked cancel. If I don't cancel, I will receive 6 brand-new novels every month, before they're available in stores! In the U.S.A., bill me at the bargain price of $3.34 plus 25¢ shipping and handling per book and applicable sales tax, if any*. In Canada, bill me at the bargain price of $3.74 plus 25¢ shipping and handling per book and applicable taxes**. That's the complete price and a savings of at least 10% off the cover prices—what a great deal! I understand that accepting the 2 free books and gift places me under no obligation ever to buy any books. I can always return a shipment and cancel at any time. Even if I never buy another book from Silhouette, the 2 free books and gift are mine to keep forever.

225 SEN DFNS
326 SEN DFNT

Name _____ (PLEASE PRINT) _____

Address _____ Apt.# _____

City _____ State/Prov. _____ Zip/Postal Code _____

* Terms and prices subject to change without notice. Sales tax applicable in N.Y.
** Canadian residents will be charged applicable provincial taxes and GST.
   All orders subject to approval. Offer limited to one per household and not valid to
   current Silhouette Desire® subscribers.
   ® are registered trademarks of Harlequin Enterprises Limited.

DES01   ©1998 Harlequin Enterprises Limited